WHAT
WAS
LEFT OF
HER:

A Story of Ghosts

Victoria Hattersley

First published 2023
by Rowanvale Books Ltd
The Gate
Keppoch Street
Roath
Cardiff
CF24 3JW
www.rowanvalebooks.com

A CIP catalogue record for this book is available from the British Library.
ISBN: 978-1-914422-60-7
Hardback ISBN: 978-1-914422-61-4
ePUB ISBN: 978-1-914422-59-1

For Mum and Dad

I

Lucie had died.

For a few days after the call from the somewhat brusque solicitor, Cassie had tried to push the fact to the back of her mind. After all, she hadn't seen her aunt in almost twenty-five years.

Twenty-five years – that long? And so many things must have happened in the meantime, only, somehow, she couldn't quite think what they were, which perhaps meant that none of them were important.

Lucie had been the closest thing to a mother Cassie or her younger sister, Alex, had ever really had – their actual mother having been gone too long for either of them to remember her, except for fragile, wispy fragments sometimes, like flickers from an old film reel. Not Lucie. Lucie was most definitely flesh and blood, looking as she had like some movie star from the 1950s. Like Ava Gardner, Cassie had thought, when she'd once seen a picture of her in a magazine.

But then, of course, there had also been Bella.

People said their cousin Bella was *wrong.* Like it was a thing you'd know – like it was as obvious and indisputable as the way the cliffs on that line of coast were falling into the sea, bit by bit, year by year. During those long summers staying with Aunt Lucie in the big house in Norfolk by the edge of the North Sea, she had come to the realisation that there was a kind of invisible barrier around her cousin that separated her from other people. The locals in the shop down the road or in the town who instinctively kept a wide berth when they saw her; the kids on the beach who hung back in groups to snigger and whisper. Those whispers and mutterings had washed around Cassie like the sound of the sea in the early morning.

There'd only been four of those summers by the sea with Lucie – just four – but somehow it had felt like more, in the way that childhood memories do: they take on significance purely because of their place in your own chronology. In the intervening years, Cassie had tried to push them away. Only, as any fool knows, memories have a way of working their way to the surface. Memories have claws.

So now here she was, that afternoon in early July, standing looking up at her aunt's house and feeling the soft, warm breeze playing over her bare arms.

The journey in the car from London was almost precisely the same as she remembered it from her childhood – the only difference being that she was the driver, not the passenger, and it wasn't her father dropping her and Alex off before going away for the summer with whatever pseudo-stepmother was on the scene. The familiar pockmarked road snaked its way through the small market town with its chip shops and antique emporiums and local convenience stores before breaking out along the lonely stretch of coast with the sea on one side and a flat landscape of fields on the other.

The house stood on its own at the top of the cliff, set apart from the scattering of '50s-built semis that clustered apologetically a few hundred yards down the road. It was tall and thin and somewhat severe, like a face that had been tested by the weather. Some faces mellow with time, others don't; this house was the latter – a three-storeyed Victorian edifice with a pointed roof, whipped year-round by the wind and the salt spray, reached by a sandy track along which only a few bits of parched, useless scrub had ever managed to grow. You had to crane your neck to see the very top floor and the pointed eaves above the attic. Doing this now sent an electric jolt up Cassie's spine that made her wince.

Not eighteen anymore. Nothing like it.

Had the brickwork always been crumbling in the way it was now? For a moment, the shabbiness of it bothered her, but then she asked herself, who really cared? It was only a house, and a house is not forever.

It was the right decision to come here, she told herself firmly. She'd *had* to do this. She closed her eyes for a moment to feel her breath go all the way down to her feet, like you were supposed to. *Breathe it in – hold it... hold it – breathe it out; don't worry about any of the other stuff right now; observe it, let it go.*

It's all bollocks, of course. You can't let it go.

She opened her eyes and looked up at the building again. The windows were dirty, like eyes obscured by cataracts. Wasn't that woman, Mrs Gibbett, supposed to be taking care of this kind of thing? Where was she, anyway? She was meant to be here to give Cassie the key. Once again, Cassie wished they'd just sent her one in the post instead – the people, the solicitors, whoever handled this kind of thing.

(That brusque solicitor who couldn't tell her precisely what had happened to Lucie to make her die, other than it had been a 'fall', as though that word explained everything...)

She gazed up again at the big sash window on the second floor, where Lucie's bedroom had been, putting her hand above her eyes to shield them from the sun and brush her hair from her face, and in that moment, she saw a pale face looking out at her. Then, just as quickly as she saw it, it was gone. If that was Mrs Gibbett inside doing some last-minute tidying, then surely she must have seen Cassie now and she'd soon be down to give her the key.

From somewhere out over the sea came the harsh shriek of a seagull. Cassie shivered, despite the warmth of the sun. Her feet were numb, stiff – almost certainly from being in the car so long. She could hardly feel the ground beneath her feet, and that bothered her, so she stomped on the gravel as though this would somehow tell her shorted-out brain to wake them up.

She startled at a noise – something had fallen around the side of the house. She craned her neck in time to see a huge ginger cat jump down from the wall surrounding the back garden. It looked fed, if not exactly cared-for, with long, orange-and-white fur and a white splodge on its forehead. Cassie didn't like or dislike cats any more than she liked or disliked most animals – or people if it came to that – but she found herself crouching carefully down in the warm gravel and holding out her hand to call it over. It looked at her for a few moments, apparently considering this overture she was making, but in the end decided to stay put and clean its paws.

There was a crunching sound behind her, and a shadow fell over her still-outstretched hand. She stood up hastily and turned around, like she'd been caught in the middle of something shameful – a kind of momentary weakness.

And there she was – Mrs Gibbett. Same thick, solid trunk built to withstand the cold winter winds that came from across the sea; same square, doughy face with small eyes that seemed to see everything and nothing. Sensible, country clothes. Sturdy. Dependable. Impassive. Hard to tell exactly how old she was, but she'd always been here, living in a small cottage at the foot of the cliff track, and before that her parents had lived there; that's what Lucie had told Cassie once. Part of the place, part of the sea and the sand and the rocks. She wasn't a friend of Lucie's exactly, but she'd often been around – coming in to 'help out', whatever that meant, and sometimes staying to drink tea and talk seemingly endlessly. Immovable, that's what she was. When everything else around her had washed into the sea, she'd probably still be there.

'Hello, Cassandra, my dear. Well, that's typical. I'm so sorry, I've been inside for ages waiting – hours, I think – and the one time I pop back to my place to get something, you arrive. But you're here now, anyway. How nice to have someone living in the house again.'

She had a deep, almost husky voice with a faint Norfolk twang that she had clearly taken pains to keep at bay, for reasons of her own.

'Really, it's fine,' said Cassie. 'I've only just got here. Actually, I thought I saw you up there in the window, but it must have been my eyes playing tricks on me. The sun's so bright.'

'Yes... although that may have been your sister, of course,' said the woman. 'We were beginning to wonder if you'd had an accident.'

Cassie frowned.

'My sister?'

'Yes. Alexandra and I were sitting waiting for you in the kitchen, having a good chat about the old days. It's been a nice change for me, I don't mind saying. Some very decent souls around here, but a lot of them are a bit limited if you want to know the truth.'

Cassie rarely wanted to know the truth, if it be told, but, in any case, she was only half listening. Instead, she was looking at the person who had just emerged from the kitchen door around the side of the house. *Alex.*

'Hello, Cassie,' Alex said. 'Surprise.'

Alex's eyes didn't leave her face, as though trying to read her reaction. There was a faint suggestion of triumph in Alex's pixieish highlights and shades, hazel eyes gleaming unsettlingly under a blunt-cut, blonde fringe.

'Hello, Alex. I didn't know you'd be coming here. Not so soon, anyway.'

'I couldn't let you go through Lucie's things all on your own, Cass. I thought we should do it together. Symbolic, sort of, don't you think?'

'How did you find out I was coming today?'

'Ah, I have my ways. You know that.'

Indeed.

The Gibbett woman was looking from one to the other of them, like she was waiting for something. She couldn't, of course, be reasonably expected to understand the things that were being said underneath the words.

'Well, aren't you going to give me a hug?' said Alex. 'I've missed you, Cass; it's been over a year.'

'Longer than that.'

Alex danced forward and folded her arms around Cassie, who returned the hug stiffly. Most of the time, Cassie felt her height to be an advantage more than anything else, yet next to Alex with her porcelain-doll frame, she felt awkward, ungainly, like some kind of praying mantis, and it brought her hurtling back to when she was a teenager. Her sister was barely five foot one, but, even so, it had always seemed to Cassie that there was far too *much* of her. She released herself as soon as she could and moved back. They looked at each other for a long moment.

'Well,' Alex finally said, too brightly. 'Shall we go in?'

'Go on, then.'

'Any bags to bring in?' said the woman behind them – Cassie had forgotten her for a moment. 'No, it's no trouble really. You've had a long drive and I'm strong – look at me. Solid arms, these.'

Cassie looked. Thick arms, thick legs, square body.

'Thanks, that's kind of you but you really don't have to.'

'No trouble at all, as I said.'

Then something occurred to Cassie and she turned back to Alex. 'You've just been in the kitchen, you said? Not upstairs?'

'Just chatting away.' Alex repeated the woman's words from earlier but with a gleeful undertone of mockery. 'Why?'

'No reason.'

Alex went ahead into the house, Mrs Gibbett following behind, hunched over Cassie's two expensive suitcases. Back in the old days, the woman had always been followed around by a yapping terrier with most of its teeth missing – until that one, unfortunate day, of course, but Cassie wasn't going to think about that now.

Just before she followed them, she turned and shielded her eyes to look at the sea just over the cliff, calm this afternoon, glittering in the sunshine. But in winter it would be mercilessly, heart-freezingly cold. And for a second, in the glimmering light, she imagined a figure standing on the edge of the cliff looking out over to the shoreline with its back to her, rigid and hostile.

Bella.

She quickly shook the thought away. And anyway, one day the sea would be all the way up here and then the house would fall into it and that would be that. Erosion. Happens to everyone and everything.

2

Through the side door that opened directly into the long kitchen and then, just like that, she was in Lucie's house again and the years since she'd been here last were swallowed up as though they'd never happened. She turned away from the others, pretending to examine the things on the shelves. Lucie's things – her painted china and her hand-painted cloth on the table and her pictures from far-flung places, which, like her, didn't quite seem to fit with their surroundings because they were too colourful, too bright; just *too*. It smelled of her, even – exotic perfume and vaguely scented lipsticks and rich, spiced food – as though she'd just stepped out for a few moments. Except, when Cassie peered a little closer, she could see what looked like the beginnings of black mould in the corner, just above the painting on the far wall of a woman in a red dress dancing on the street outside a café.

And Cassie was mildly put out to find that somehow, in the short time they'd been waiting for her, the other two had managed to strike up something of a rapport. Alex got tea ready like the lady of the house; Mrs Gibbett, having deposited the bags in the hallway, sat down at the table and showed no signs of leaving.

'Sit down, Cassandra, my dear,' said the woman. 'You must be so tired after that long journey.'

She made it sound as though Cassie had come from the other side of the world, not down the A11 from London.

'Mrs Gibbett's been telling me about the carnival in town next month,' said Alex as she crashed the teapot onto the table. 'She's going to have a stall; she's going to *sell* things.'

Only Cassie could detect the delightedly mocking gleam in Alex's Bambi eyes. Her mouth was slightly open, her upper lip a perfect Cupid's bow, the lower looking like it was about to be bitten in excitement at any moment. She felt the familiar surge of terrible protectiveness mixed with an irritation that she sometimes thought bordered on the pathological. Why did she feel it wasn't *safe* for Alex to be here? Why did she want her to be far, far away? Had Lucie felt the same about her own younger sister, their mother? If so, going far away hadn't made any difference in the end...

Cassie cast her eyes to the ceiling (damp spots – as though the house was dribbling all down itself like a sick person in a hospital bed) and took a deep breath.

She's here now; nothing you can do about it. She has every right to be, after all.

'Really?' she said, turning to Mrs Gibbett. 'What kind of stall?'

'It's just something we're doing during the carnival to help raise funds to mend the church roof in town because, oh, it's in a dreadful state – falling to bits, in fact, like lots of things around here. You should really both come along, I said to Alexandra; I think you'd enjoy it. You'd feel like you were part of things again after all this time and then...'

Blocking out the woman's voice, Cassie stared out of the window at the dune path leading down to the sea. She thought about grief, and how in the short time since she'd heard about Lucie, hers seemed to have manifested in nightmares rather than weeping or any of the usual things people – *normal* people with *normal* feelings – were supposed to do. Over the past two or three weeks she'd been waking up at night crouched on the other side of her room, heart beating and covered in cold sweat with a shadow looming over her. Loss was a faceless figure in the dark, and even though the dreams and the figure were only in her head, they felt different.

They felt real.

You can't even grieve like a proper person – that's what Alex would have said to her, if Cassie had told her. But then, why should she, she thought with a sudden surge of resentment, when Lucie had made herself absent from her life for so long? And why had Lucie even *been* here to have this unspecified accident? If things had happened the way they should have, then her aunt ought to have been long gone from this place. She'd never belonged here. Never. She clenched the first of her left hand – the weak one, the one that sometimes shook – and dug her nails in until her palm burned.

She was drawn back to the room by Mrs Gibbett, who'd finally finished her monologue.

'Well, listen at me chatting here when I've got things to be getting on with and you want to get settled in. Look at you, Cassandra – you're so tired after the journey you can barely speak. I'll leave you to it.'

'I'm not so tired,' she said. 'It's just strange to be here, I suppose, after all these years. I – we – didn't even know Lucie was living here again; somehow I'd been under the impression she'd gone away after Bella... How long had she been back for?'

'Oh, goodness – a few years at least. You know how time goes.'

Years? Cassie looked at Alex, but her sister seemed to be absorbed with her pink-painted toenails.

'Did she say anything about why she'd come back again? I thought, perhaps, because of all those friends she once had...'

She hated that this woman was the only person she could ask these questions of. *Hated* it.

'Oh, it wasn't for me to ask. Of course, I'm surprised she didn't get in touch with you, but then—'

'The man I spoke to said Lucie hadn't wanted a funeral, and we don't even know where her ashes are.'

Mrs Gibbett's face screwed up in something like distress and she bashed herself on the side of the head.

'Oh, of course – so thoughtless of me not to have told you about your aunt's ashes. Whatever must you think? They're on the sideboard in the sitting room, dear, on the high shelf in a lovely urn. One that belonged to your aunt – she brought it with her when she came back home; so tasteful, of course.'

'She brought an *urn* back with her?'

'Yes. Lovely thing.'

'Alright... Thank you.'

Mrs Gibbett shook her heavy head and pulled herself up and then, just before she left, she turned back to Cassie and said:

'You know, it's amazing how much you look like your aunt. Longer hair, of course, but your face – you could be her. Same green eyes and everything. Same way of holding yourself tall. Funny.'

She stood there looking at Cassie for just a moment longer than was comfortable, and then shook her head and bustled out. Suddenly, the two sisters were left sitting opposite each other at the table with a heavy silence hanging between them like a body swinging on a noose. Cassie sensed that Alex was annoyed at the woman's parting remark, and she allowed herself to feel a momentary quiet pleasure.

'Why do you keep looking at me like that, Cass?'

'Like what?'

'Like there's something wrong with me. You've been doing it since you got here.'

Alex's fingers were twisting together on the table, her foot tapping. Why could she never just be *still*?

'I didn't realise I was. I suppose I wasn't expecting you Al, that's all.'

'Well, why not? It's my house too; Lucie left it to *both* of us.'

'I know that – you don't have to tell me. Did you think I was trying to keep her – it – for myself?'

'So, is it over between you and Jon, then? Has he left the flat?'

'*I* left the flat. And we were never really much of a thing.'

'Dad would have helped you out with a new place. You didn't have to come here if it makes you look so miserable.'

Ask Daddy: the answer to everything. Cassie would never ask Daddy again though – not now she didn't have to. Hadn't seen him in over two years, or maybe longer. He'd always been happy to leave them here – the two motherless whelps – for weeks on end during those long-ago summers, whether they liked it or not. And the funny thing was she could tell that he didn't really like Lucie. That he was probably the only person who didn't, in fact. Maybe, she'd thought – ever the perceptive child – that he resented her aunt in some way for being alive when Cassie's mother wasn't; for being more able to bear whatever it was about their dour, bleak childhood in this place that couldn't be borne. He'd loved their mother as much as he was able to love anyone, she supposed, but it seemed any real interest he'd had in his daughters had gone with her – and really, that was fine with Cassie, just not for Alex. Oh, how Alex wanted to be Daddy's girl.

'I didn't want him to help me out. Anyway, I didn't come here because I *had* to. I wouldn't – we couldn't have some stranger going through Lucie's things even if she didn't bother contacting us.'

Yes, that's why she was here. To do the usual things that you do when someone dies. Sort through the ashes of their life and tidy them away. That was all – nothing more.

Alex shrugged. 'I don't know why you won't ask him for anything. May as well get something out of him, that's what I've always said.'

'Oh, I know that. So how long are you staying, anyway?'

Alex smiled – somewhat maliciously, Cassie thought.

'I'll stay as long as you do – longer, maybe. This is a big house and there's plenty of room for the both of us. Anyway, how long are *you* going to stay? Don't you have work on – commissions or whatever?'

'I'm taking a break from work.'

There was a bitter taste in her mouth, something in the air, maybe. She put her hands on the table, pushing herself to her feet.

'Well, I'm going to take my things upstairs. Which room are you in?'

'The one I always stayed in, of course.'

Cassie went out into the hallway where Mrs Gibbett had left her cases. Standing at the foot of the wide staircase that led to the first floor, she looked up to the high, narrow window at the top of the landing. Next to it was the window seat where Lucie had liked to sit, looking out at the beach and beyond it to places only she could see, her eyes restless, her body shifting. She could never stay still, just like Alex in that way (although Cassie could admit to herself that she didn't like the comparison).

Why do you stay here? Cassie had thought. *You don't belong here.* Sometimes Lucie would turn to her with a sad smile on her red lips as though she'd heard the silent question.

Again, she caught the faint whiff of perfume in the air. Funny how a person's scent can stay in a place after so long, almost as though it has a life independent of them.

(*Did she scream when she had this 'fall'? Did she fall far? Was her body broken? Did she lie on the ground in a pool of blood? If I'd been there and stood over her, would her eyes have opened and looked up...? Stop it.*)

Next to her was the grandfather clock: Grandad Maddon's clock. The only thing of his Lucie had kept after he'd finally died – some time before the first summer they'd come here. Everything else of his had been chucked, burned, like she'd wanted to erase him. When they'd come here that first time, there had still been scorch marks at the end of the garden where she'd lit the big fire. So now there was just this one object, tall and proud and severe like the house itself. Once, when Cassie had asked Lucie why she'd kept only the clock, she'd laughed a strange little laugh and told her it was a reminder that everything comes to an end except time, because time isn't really real. And while she did it, she'd twisted the chunky bracelet on her left arm that hid an old scar, and that's when Cassie had got the thought that perhaps inheritance comes in many forms...

There was an ornate mirror next to the clock – there were mirrors all over the house. Lucie hadn't been vain, but... They gave the illusion that the place was even bigger than it was. Cassie looked into the glass and remembered Mrs Gibbett's last comment as she studied her own face. Was Lucie – lovely Lucie – in there, in her own pale cheeks and green eyes?

She couldn't see it herself, much as she'd have liked to.

***

The room she'd always slept in overlooked the garden and the sea beyond the cliffs. Further along the shoreline she could just make out the shape of an old beach hut that she was pretty sure had been there when she was a child.

She turned away from the view, across the landing to Alex's room. The door was open to reveal the old iron bedstead and the floor already covered in clothes as though they'd been hastily thrown down or someone had turned the place over.

She stepped back out onto the landing. A shaft of afternoon light had fallen through the tall window at the top of the stairs. The landing stretched off on both sides of the stairwell. One side, to the right, led to Lucie's room and a couple of other guest rooms. On the other side, if you turned left from Alex's room, there was another hallway that led to Bella's room and the bathroom. And then, right at the end, the door to the attic stairs.

A sudden blast of some kind of '80s cock rock – possibly Whitesnake – came from downstairs. It seemed a jarring obscenity in a house that had so long sat empty, like a burst of laughter at a funeral. Alex must have found a radio; she'd already complained about the lack of internet, so they were clearly at the mercy of whatever local station she'd tuned into. How very 1990s.

Cassie took a couple of hesitant steps towards her aunt's room, before stopping to close her eyes for a moment. *Grow up, Cassie*, said the now-familiar, vicious, chiding voice inside her head. She took a breath, held up her chin and forced her legs to carry her towards the closed door at the end of the landing.

Lucie's room was just as it had ever been; that was the first thing she noticed – like she'd just stepped out for a moment and she'd be back soon. There was the huge oak wardrobe holding her beautiful, expensive, well-cut dresses ('vintage', they'd call them now; they'd probably go for a fortune on-line). Her perfume on the dressing table and jewellery hanging either side of the mirror. A single ornament stood on the mantelpiece: a carved stone bust of a woman that looked a bit like Lucie – made or given to her by a long-gone admirer, perhaps. It was starting to crumble a little around the face in a way that Cassie found disquieting.

She closed her eyes again and deliberately took herself back to that long-ago time; Lucie sitting at the antique dressing table she'd loved so much, fixing pearl earrings into her ears even though she'd never be going anywhere special, just for the pleasure of it, tilting her face up so the light bounced off her high cheekbones. Cassie would be perched on the edge of the high-backed chair next to the window, watching Lucie get ready. For what? Dinner? Maybe it was one of those few times she'd had people come to stay, bohemian friends from another part of her life – rich pretend-hippies who played guitar and laughed a lot and asked her when she was going to leave this place and come back to where she belonged, wherever that was. And Lucie'd just laughed too and said, *all in good time. This is just temporary.*

Oh, Cassie could remember these things alright. She could remember details from twenty, thirty years ago; she could remember lying in her crib at a few months old and looking up at the ceiling. She just sometimes, these days, forgot what had happened yesterday, or what she'd walked into a room to do.

Lucie's voice had been deep, with a hint of gravel, a bit like her own. If anyone had asked Cassie what her favourite thing about herself was, she'd have said it was this voice that she shared with her aunt. As she opened her eyes, Cassie could hear it even now, across the years, playing over her and down her spine.

'*How do you get your hair like that, Lucie?*'

'*Oh, years of practice, darling.*'

'*Are we always going to come here?*'

'*Of course, as long as I'm here, and longer if you want.*'

Memories. What were they worth in the end? She would not be held hostage by the past and she would not be afraid of absence. What was it Lucie had said to her, in one of those many times they'd sat together in this room in the early evenings? Something about being what you had to be and not letting the past eat you up.

'*You know, the way you stop the past swallowing you whole is by taking charge of your future.*'

But then, Cassie couldn't believe Lucie's future had turned out the way she'd have written it.

There was a sudden flash, right in the corner of her left eye, in the doorway, like something had moved. Most likely her eyes playing tricks on her, like she'd said to Mrs Gibbett. It happened more and more often these days; sometimes Cassie felt there was something following her around, and she'd turn quickly to catch it, but it would be gone. Unless...

'Alex?'

She moved quickly towards the door – too quickly, probably, because as she stepped out onto the landing, her left foot scuffed the floor, catching on something, and then the ground was rising up to meet her. She just had time to put out her hands to stop her face from hitting it first, but the shock of it made her gasp. What had caught her? The corner of the rug? A nail sticking out the floorboard?

She breathed deep, marvelling at how a sudden fall takes you instantly back to childhood, when you'd be running and then there'd come the abrupt plunge and the tears. The breath turned into a harsh cough as the dust she'd disturbed flew into her throat; the floor smelled bad, and now she was breathing it in. The house *tingled;* she could feel it vibrating through the floor against her skin, and up close, she could see that some of the boards around the edge of the rug had woodworm and bits were rotting away. There was something shiny stuck in between the boards, and she pushed her fingers in to get it out, crumbling away some of the wood as she did so. A shock of pain brought tears to her eyes for a moment.

It was one of Lucie's earrings: a single pearl, clean and delicate with a little post that had jabbed straight under the nail of her middle finger. She looked beyond the earring at her outstretched hands, at her long fingers that darling, spiteful Alex always said were like spider legs. They looked wrong, suddenly; twisted. Her vision swam for a moment, and she held her breath as she watched her hands distort and take on a sort of red glow. *Crab claws.* Where had that thought come from?

This is how people die. They fall and nobody comes to find them and they lie there for days in a Gothic mess on the floor and eventually people find them and describe how awful the smell was and one day someone makes a documentary about it.

And then, as she lay there, she heard, just for a moment, a scratching sound. It was coming from above her.

Are there mice?

A door opened downstairs and the music got louder. She blinked her eyes back into focus.

'Cassie? Did you call me?'

She pushed herself up on to her knees and slipped the earring into her pocket. Alex mustn't know. Somehow that seemed important, like it would put her at a disadvantage.

She was coming up the stairs now.

'Why are you sitting on the landing?'

'This rug needs cleaning.'

'Well, probably. There's a funny smell in the house. Do you think it's cat piss?'

'No.'

'Bella's room is empty.'

'What?'

'All her things are gone, even the bed.'

'So?'

'I'm just saying. Come down anyway. There're some nibbly bits I brought with me and I've made us drinks; I bet you didn't bring anything at all. Let's toast Lucie.'

Cassie sighed and hauled herself to her feet. At the top of the stairs, she glanced along the other side of the landing, at the door to the attic at the end of it, and then just as quickly looked away.

She followed her sister down the stairs.

3

Alex, rather ghoulishly in Cassie's opinion, had made some kind of cocktail with the half-empty bottles in Lucie's drinks cabinet. ('They've only been sitting there gathering dust – might as well use them. It's what Lucie would want.') The result was faintly sour and gravelly, and Cassie thought it was what age must taste like. Alex had turned the radio off now, so they sat together in silence for a while in the living room, which stretched the entire length of the house. The French windows were open onto the back garden. Cassie listened to the sea and watched the light slowly fade from the day, the shadows lengthening on the lawn, which was cut off abruptly, jaggedly, by the crumbling cliff at the end. Years ago, Lucie had put fairy lights out in the garden, and Alex and Cassie would sit out there listening while Lucie played her records or, sometimes, the piano. The *Moonlight Sonata* had been a favourite. Occasionally she'd let Alex and Cassie have a glass of wine with her. Happier days.

Cassie reminded herself, again, that there was no point in being hostile to Alex. The voice of the house-mistress from the expensive boarding school came back to her: *'She is your sister, after all. Surely you have some sway with her; surely you can reason with her a bit.'* You would think so, wouldn't you, Miss Hathaway?

'You know, Cass, I've been thinking – we couldn't sell this place even if we wanted to, the way the cliffs are falling away. You'd have to be mad to buy it.'

Sometimes Alex gave the disturbing impression of reading her thoughts.

'We could rent it out in the future, maybe? To people going on holiday?'

'If people do that here.'

'We did.'

'It was different for us. We were unwanted waifs.'

They both sat in silence again for a moment, but Alex could never keep quiet for long.

'Cass?'

'What?'

'Is that the urn with Lucie's ashes? That big china pot with all the decoration on it?'

Alex pointed to the urn on the high shelf above the drinks cabinet.

'How many other urns do you see in here?'

Cassie had been actively trying not to look at it with its ornate decoration ('so tasteful') and its demand to be seen.

'Do you think we should think of somewhere to scatter the ashes?'

'Sometime, of course we should. There's no rush, is there?'

There was another silence while they both drank. Cassie looked down again at the book she was holding but not taking in, and then:

'Cass?'

'*What?*'

'Why *did* Lucie stay here so long?'

'What do you mean?'

But Cassie knew only too well what she meant, because she'd thought it for as long as she had known her aunt.

'I don't think I properly noticed it at the time, but she didn't *fit* here, did she? She could have gone anywhere or done anything with anyone. I mean, she'd been all over the place, hadn't she, only to end up back here with the grandparents and have a *baby* of all things. If she really wanted a baby, why'd she come back here to do it? I mean, she hated Grandad Maddon, didn't she? That's what Dad said. She and Mum both hated him and they hated it here.'

'Yes, well, what we really know about our mother wouldn't fill the back of an envelope.'

Of course, Cassie had once asked Lucie that – why she had stayed here in this big, lonely house. And she could hear Lucie's voice in her head now, through the years.

'Now that's a question. Well, I was going to have your cousin, of course, and my, didn't that make your grandfather angry when I came back here, an unmarried woman with a baby on the way. That sort of thing mattered around here back then – to someone like him, anyway. And of course, your grandma had gone by then so he had to disapprove all by himself.' She'd smiled, as though the very sight of that had been worth the years since – only, the smile had stayed in her mouth and didn't travel up to her eyes.

Cassie had asked about their mother once, but she'd never done it again because Lucie had looked too sad.

'I should have looked out for her more when she was younger. She was more fragile than me, you see; I think in the end the past caught up with her, poor Maggie. We argued a bit, of course, just like you and Alex do now and then – like all sisters do. But I don't think I ever loved anyone as much. You and Alex should look out for each other, you know.'

Cassie loved the way Lucie talked to her like she was a fellow conspirator, not a child – it was one of the things that made them special. Her face had gone far away, Cassie remembered. She wondered now whether Bella's unnamed father, who'd never been around, had been someone Lucie missed or just someone she would rather forget. Nobody had known who he was; some had said he was 'probably foreign'. In any case, there had been no need to have Bella and be a mother all by herself, even then, if she really hadn't wanted to, as Cassie herself knew only too well... She thought of Grandad Maddon and one of the few things she remembered her father saying to Lucie when he'd dropped Cassie and Alex off and thought they weren't listening.

'I see you burned the old bastard's things. If it were up to me, the house would have burned with him in it years ago.'

Somehow it was one of the realest things she'd ever heard him say. It was the closest she'd come to seeing him as a person.

And so, the answer to Alex's question came to her.

'I think she came back so she could see him die and she could be sure he'd gone.'

'See who die?'

'Grandad Maddon.'

Very Cassie. Very matter of fact.

'You don't really think that?'

'And then, of course, Bella turned out to be... difficult... and maybe it was just... easier to stay, for a while.'

Maybe she'd told herself that she'd leave when she could. But sometimes people stay just that little bit too long. Sometimes people stay until it's too late and then they fall apart until there's nothing left of what they were.

Alex shivered and hugged her legs up towards herself in her childlike way.

'Bella. I don't like thinking about her.' She shook her head, as though trying to get rid of her. 'But anyway, did you ever see Lucie even *talk* to anyone from around here, except that damn woman from down the road?'

'You mean your friend Mrs Gibbett?'

'Oh, I was just having a laugh with her.'

'You shouldn't encourage her. I know people like that, she won't bloody go away. She never did years ago, always hovering around in the wings and dropping in – I'm surprised it didn't drive Lucie mad. I don't think I've ever once heard her say anything remotely interesting.'

Alex sighed heavily and swallowed the rest of the revolting cocktail.

'I've always missed Lucie. I *loved* coming here. I was closer to her than anyone else was, you know. She was like me, didn't want to be ordinary.'

Cassie said nothing. And really, she and Alex should have hated staying here summer after summer – not much to do, nothing like the city they were used to. But it wasn't like that, because there had been Lucie. Lucie had felt like home. And there was a kind of freedom here, because here they could stay up as long as they wanted, go out alone all day if they wanted to and they'd be safe. True, there had been Bella, but most of the time she had kept to herself, a slight, disquieting figure wandering along the shore for hours on end, wading through the water looking for dead things, or retreating to the attic to think whatever dark thoughts went through that head of hers.

'What was that?'

Alex's voice jolted her back to the present.

'What was what?'

'Something in the garden.'

Alex moved towards the open French windows for a closer look and then gave a scream as the large ginger cat from earlier leapt onto the piano stool. Cassie laughed in spite of herself.

'It's not shy, is it?' said Alex, her hand over her heart, laughing, too, now.

The cat was purring and cleaning itself, calm as anything, but watching them out of one eye.

'I'm going to see if there's anything I can give it to eat.'

Alex went into the kitchen, and Cassie looked at the cat.

'Don't get yourself too comfortable here,' she said.

Cats always stared at her, but this one looked more inquisitive than hostile, so she didn't mind it too much.

Without thinking what she was doing, she leaned over and stretched out her fingers to the cat for the second time that day. It sniffed her, and this time it butted her hand graciously with its head. Cassie stroked it and found that its fur was thick, warm and slightly coarse. And as she did so, she had a proper look at Lucie's piano. The cover had been left up, exposing yellowing keys inlaid with the grime of a thousand fingers. It was mostly dark brown, except the left side of it, the one facing the window, which had been faded by the sunlight. It looked old. It looked, in fact, as though it could have been sitting in that spot for at least a century. Underneath it there would be spiders and dead mice and cobwebs with listed status.

She'd practised on this piano, during those summer days – it was another thing she and Lucie had shared and Alex hadn't. (Alex had never had the patience to learn an instrument.) They'd played duets, sometimes, their long fingers working side by side, the bangles on Lucie's left arm clanking together.

Something caught her eye on top of the piano. A framed photo of three people on the beach – Lucie, Cassie and Alex. She remembered now how Lucie had asked a passerby to take it. *We must have meant something to her, then, mustn't we, if she kept this all those years?* In the picture, Cassie had on her cut-off jeans and baggy T-shirt – pretty much the only thing she'd ever worn. Her legs looked skinny, coltish. Next to her, Alex was wearing a little floral skirt and a cut-off vest top. Jailbait. Lucie had on some kind of '50s-style summer dress cinched in at the waist. She had her arms around them both, a dazzling smile on her face, and she was really the only thing your eye was drawn to.

Then Cassie saw there was a fourth person, but in the background like she'd been pushed out of the picture. Bella, in that blue dress of hers that had got too small for her, her eyes peeping out malevolently from under that jagged fringe. For the first time, Cassie realised how much Bella resembled Lucie; a smaller, paler, thinner version, of course, with different coloured eyes, but the same shaped face, the same high cheekbones. Bella's hands were behind her back, but if they'd been in view, Cassie knew they would be raw, red, peeling from constantly being dipped in the cold sea and that incessant biting. Bella's hands had been like the claws of dead crabs and other assorted detritus she collected endlessly and obsessively as they washed up on the beach each day.

She heard her own voice then, from across the years. Hard, bitter. She'd been angry with Bella about something that day, hadn't she?

'No, Bella, you can't be in this one. This is just for us.'

She'd been a child, maybe, but not a young child. Twelve? Thirteen? Old enough to be kinder, or at least pretend to be.

Alex bounded back into the room and Cassie put the picture down.

'Here, puss, I've brought you some cheese.' She knelt and held out a piece, coaxingly.

'I'm not sure cats eat brie.'

But Alex stubbornly held it out, and, eventually, the cat came up to sniff it. Alex stroked the cat while it ate, ruffling its ears and head in the way that everybody – even Cassie – knew cats hated.

When the cat finished eating, Alex sat back on the sofa, picked it up and deposited it on her lap.

'Aren't you supposed to wait for them to come to you?' said Cassie.

But Alex was stroking the cat and, gallingly, it seemed happy enough to settle down. This pissed Cassie off more than perhaps it needed to. She drained the last of her drink with a hand that, she noticed with distaste, shook ever so slightly.

'Let's give her a name,' said Alex, looking sideways at Cassie.

'The cat?'

'Yes. I'm going to christen her Lucie.'

'We're not calling the cat Lucie. It's not even our cat, and how do you know it's a girl?'

'Of course she's a girl, and she looks like a Lucie. Sort of regal, you know. Beautiful.'

Alex continued to stroke the cat's head. The only sounds were its deep purr and the occasional piercing shriek of a seagull outside.

Cassie was suddenly exhausted. Done with the day and what it had held. She'd forgotten what an unsettling person her sister was to be around, like an unexploded bomb. Again, the feeling, *it's not safe for Alex to be here. She should be far away; maybe I should too, if it comes to that.*

'I'm going upstairs.'

'It's only half ten. What's the matter with you? I've hardly seen you for the past two years.'

'Bloody hell – I'm tired, that's all. It's been a long day and I want some time to myself.'

'That's *all* you have from what I can see,' muttered Alex.

'What?'

'Oh, nothing. Anyway, please yourself – you always do. I'm going to have another drink or several.'

***

Cassie was about to push open her bedroom door when she heard the scratching again – faint, but unmistakably there. She stood still, listening for the source of the sound. It was hard to tell now if it was above or below, but it seemed to be coming from the other end of the landing, near Bella's room or the attic.

It was childish not to want to go over there; she'd have to eventually. She went to the light switch outside Alex's room and flicked it on so the landing burst into life, dappled with shadows from the delicate, ornate gold lampshade suspended over the stairwell. She padded along the landing, past the bathroom, and pushed open the door to Bella's room. The light in there didn't work, but Alex was right; it was clearly empty, the floor uncarpeted. It was like somebody had wanted to erase Bella's presence.

Bella hated us. Hated us coming here. Hated me.

The scratching again, louder now, and definitely coming from above. *Fucking hell,* Cassie thought. If it was mice, they'd be chewing things, eating cables, shorting out circuits, making holes. She'd have to investigate it while she was here.

Then, just as suddenly as it had started, the sound stopped. She waited for a moment before turning and heading back along the landing to her room. That was when she saw the shape in the corner of her eye again, standing in front of the tall window at the top of the stairs. It was only there for a second, but when she turned to face it, it was gone and she told herself, as she always did, that it was nothing at all.

She went into her room where she rummaged in one of her suitcases and drew out a bottle of vodka. She rummaged further to find the pills, and then swallowed one, washing it down with a long gulp of the burning alcohol. With a sigh she'd been holding in all evening, she stretched out full length on the bed with the bottle still in her hand, staring out at the blue-black sky.

She lay there, and in the stillness, she felt the house tingle.

4

It was the scratching again.

Or clawing? Was it, after all, more like clawing?

Cassie sat at the desk in her room trying to type, but the sound – faint though it was – refused to let her. It wasn't as though it was continuous, and in a way that was the problem. It would stop for a time, and she'd think it had gone away, only for it to start up again in what seemed like another part of the house. It could drive you mad, this kind of thing, if you were the sort of person who'd let it.

Cassie and Alex had been here for several days now, and between the two of them they'd established a routine of sorts, or at least a way of living together under one roof – something they'd not really done since they'd been kids. After that first evening, they talked very little, or rather, they talked but didn't *say* anything. Cassie still couldn't understand why Alex would choose to come to this place, with no crowds of people around to admire her and laugh at the things she said. And despite their ostensible reason for being here – sorting through Lucie's things – Alex seemed as reluctant to start on it as Cassie.

Another one of those momentary flashes in the corner of her eye. Automatically she turned her head to look at it – to catch it before it went away – but as usual she was too slow. People in the online sick-people communities she'd visited said nobody will believe you when these things happen, they'll think you're making it up, so a lot of the time you're best keeping it to yourself, otherwise they'll say you're losing it – whatever *it* is.

Then there was a thud to the other side of her. She turned to see Lucie the cat had jumped down from the bed. *Woken up, finally. I'm glad someone can sleep soundly.* Cassie had never had a cat on her bed before coming here, but she found it surprisingly comforting, so she let Lucie stay.

Scratch, scratch, scratch.

'You should be dealing with that,' she said to Lucie.

The cat said nothing, naturally. She stretched before curling her way around the door and out onto the landing.

Cassie pushed the cover of her laptop down and stood up.

***

There were muffled voices behind the closed kitchen door. Mrs Gibbett again, of course, sitting at the table for all the world as though she belonged there. Almost every day, she seemed to find a reason to materialise.

'... so I thought I'd bring it over anyway – you might enjoy it or you might not. There's not much around here for a couple of single girls your age... Oh, hello, Cassandra, my dear. I just brought over these leaflets for the carnival in town in July – you remember I told you about it?'

Girls. Even Alex would have to admit that was pushing it.

'It's not all that much really, but I play my part organising, for what it's worth, and it might be a day out for you. Bit of fun. I can imagine you might be getting a little bored here. I'm used to it, but for city girls like you... How long do you think you'll be staying this time?'

Cassie looked at her little eyes, set deep in that square face. What did she want them to say? Would she like them to stay forever so she could drop in every morning for tea, or did she secretly hate – *hate* them being here? What did she *do* with her days? Lucie'd always found her tedious, hadn't she? *'Oh, here she comes again, girls.'* And yet she'd put up with her presence all the same. Why?

'We'll be there, won't we, Cass?' said Alex, fixing those big, innocent eyes on her, willing her to laugh. Cassie kept her face stubbornly, wilfully, straight.

'I'll be on my stall on the day, but I'm sure I told you about that already... Oh, get out – go on, shoo.'

Lucie the cat had come out from under the kitchen table.

'No, it's OK, we like her,' said Alex hastily. 'She's sort of become part of the family, hasn't she, Cass?'

'Oh, you're letting her in, are you? She's been hanging about the house for ages – Lord knows where she's come from – and I've been chasing her away, but I won't if you're making a pet of her. Be careful though, she might have fleas. I'd hate to think of an infestation in your aunt's lovely house.'

Cassie looked around at the walls of Lucie's house; covered with lovely things, yes, but the paper behind them was peeling nonetheless.

'Actually, talking of infestations, I've – or we've – been hearing scratching.'

('*We've?*' muttered Alex.)

'Scratching?'

'Scratching. I don't know if it's mice or something, but I thought maybe I ought to get it checked out, and I wondered if you'd ever heard anything...'

Cassie looked at the woman's face to see her reaction. She was frowning. *Yes, I know – that's the sort of thing you were being paid to keep an eye on, wasn't it?* The maliciousness of her inner voice startled even her for a moment; was this what happened to you when you got older and angrier?

'Oh goodness, I've never heard anything like that in all the times I've been in here.'

A vision now popped into Cassie's head of the woman walking around the house on her own the past year. Running her rough hands over the furniture, caressing it with dusters. Touching Lucie's things, even...

'That's one of the reasons we're quite glad to have the cat around.' No need to say that it showed no interest in the noises whatsoever.

'Well, of course – I'll contact the local pest man.'

And now the picture in Cassie's head was replaced with a grotesque array of traps and broken-necked mice littered all over the house.

'No need,' she said hastily. 'If it gets worse, we'll find someone.'

'I expect the house is haunted,' said Alex.

Cassie rolled her eyes.

The woman shook her head, looking down at the cat. 'Well, I don't know. Perhaps you'll catch a few mice, hey?'

She put her hand down to pat Lucie on the head, but Lucie, who was halfway through washing her face, turned tail and scratched at the kitchen door to be let outside. Alex got up to open it for her and then, for some reason, she followed her out into the back garden.

'Well, I was always more of a dog person myself.' Mrs Gibbett's eyes looked away for a moment.

'Of course, that's right,' said Cassie.

Oh, Jesus Christ, yes: the dog. The day Mrs Gibbett's yapping terrier died...

It had all begun with Cassie hearing a shout from downstairs. She'd run down to see the woman and Lucie rushing out of the kitchen and across the garden after Bella, who was holding the little dog in her arms and had reached the part where the cliff dropped off. Cassie had followed after them, probably more out of curiosity than anything else at that point.

'Put it down now, Bella,' Lucie had called out in her deep, clear voice. 'You've had your fun.'

'I only said young girls shouldn't speak that way to their mothers,' said Mrs Gibbett. 'Oh, look you're frightening Rexie. Put him down, there's a girl.'

Bella had just looked at her with her pale eyes, and then she'd held the dog out, quite calmly, and let it go over the cliff. Cassie remembered, after her aunt and Mrs Gibbett had rushed down there, going to the end of the garden to look over and seeing it lying small and pathetic on the rocks.

But maybe even worse than the dead dog was the look on Lucie's face. Not angry, not sad, not even shocked – just utterly resigned. Blank. *That's what she is*, said her face. *That's what I produced.*

The mug Cassie was holding slipped to the floor and smashed, as though her hand had suddenly just forgotten what it was for. Angry at herself, she crouched down to pick up the pieces, and suddenly she felt a hand on her shoulder and the words, 'Let me do that for you.' She turned to find that Mrs Gibbett was crouching behind her, too close, looking intently into her face. The woman smelled strongly of lavender, slightly sickly. She put her hand on the side of the table and pulled herself up. The woman continued to pick up the rest of the pieces and then straightened herself up. Their eyes met and Cassie felt a certain unease.

'Oh, that's a nice song, Alexandra.'

Cassie turned to see that Alex had come back into the kitchen and was humming a tune – for a moment, she struggled to place it, and then she remembered, it was one of Lucie's favourites. Lucie'd liked the old songs, '50s classics – there had been certain ones she'd played, over and over, until they'd become bound up, in Cassie's mind, with summer and childhood.

'I found Lucie's old record player in the back of a cupboard with all her records, and I was looking through them. Remember this, Cass?', and she sang the words... *I only have eyes for you, dear.*'

A song out of time and out of place. Like Lucie.

Cassie looked away, and Alex continued to hum to herself as she stood over the sink.

Finally, the woman stood up to go. 'Oh well, cheerio then. Enjoy your day.'

They watched her through the window as she walked back down the cliff to her little house.

'You encourage her,' said Cassie.

'Oh, lighten up,' said Alex. 'Are we braving the shop today, then? We're out of food and cocktail stuff.'

Cassie nodded and stood up, putting the thought of the dead dog out of her mind. It was done now. No point dwelling on the past, after all.

5

The local shop was about half a mile down the coast road between the cliff house and the town, sat in amongst a random cluster of dwellings of varying sizes, too small to be called a village or even a hamlet. There was no pavement on the side of the road, so they had to walk on the grass verge. The sea was still today, the sky sickeningly blue, and out on the water a small boat was bobbing away. The scene, as always, was too idyllic, too postcard-perfect, and Cassie felt that if you looked closely, you would see decay under the sand and on the cliff face and in the things that washed up now and then from the sea.

Now, she realised, there was a person walking along the sand in a bright summer dress, swinging their arms, and for a stupid moment she thought: *Lucie*. As she watched, the person stopped and turned to face her, as though they could feel her eyes on them. She looked away, and shivered.

Alex was walking slightly ahead in that springy, hip-swinging way of hers, like she was always on the verge of breaking into a dance.

'Come on,' she called back.

'I'm in no rush,' said Cassie.

Just before the shop, they passed the bus stop. There were signs on it advertising the upcoming carnival in town (The Crowning of the Carnival Queen! Bouncy castles! Tombolas!). Cassie found it oddly depressing that the bus stop was still intact – no smashed panes, no graffiti. Where were all the kids? There was one person there, though: about their age or maybe a bit younger, with long, thin, reddish hair pulled back in a ponytail and a crumpled dress that hung baggily on her. She had a baby over her shoulder, wrapped up in blankets even on a hot day like this. Must have come from one of those houses.

Then the woman turned her face slightly towards them, revealing a thick, faded scar down the side of her face. It brought a jolt of recognition. Cassie forced her face into an expression that she hoped was more smile than sneer – she was out of practice – and the woman looked away quickly, holding the baby closer to her and adjusting the blankets over it. It was not the time to 'claim an acquaintance', if Cassie was going to be all Jane Austen about it. She followed Alex, who had already reached the shop and pushed open the door.

It was the kind of place that sold a bit of everything, and nothing was in a logical order. The old guy behind the counter nodded as they came in.

'I think he's the same one who was here when we used to come for sweets,' said Alex in her ear.

Cassie concurred. She recognised the mole on the side of his nose, his faint whiff of tobacco mixed with penny sweets – a somewhat disturbing mixture, now she thought about it.

'Come on, let's find the booze section. They must have one,' said Alex.

They located it and were arguing half-heartedly over the limited selection of spirits when Alex stopped and nudged her.

'Look, over there near the canned crap.'

'What, that couple over there? They've been staring at us since we came in here. Perhaps they know we're the cousins of the freak.'

'Have they? They can keep looking. No, over the far end.'

Cassie looked, and then she saw him. Shaggy fair hair and a bit of a beard. Tall and kind of lean, almost extravagantly tanned. He had ripped jeans and a white T-shirt with some kind of graphic design on it. Even from here she could see there was a faint scar running down the side of one bicep, like he'd been off wrestling an alligator or something.

In short, just the kind of romance novel rough-and-ready type that her little sister would go for like a guided missile.

'Mick Dundee?'

'Don't you recognise him?'

'You're being really obvious.'

But Cassie did recognise him; of course she did.

'You must remember, Cass. I had a massive crush on him when we were kids. I remember the first time I saw him down on the beach; he was coming out of the water and it was like he had a halo around him or something, and I said to you, "I've seen God."'

Cassie had first seen him from the window of the house, and she recalled like it was yesterday, the stirrings of curiosity about this strange being going about his business (they had, after all, been at an all-girls boarding school). She'd watched him too, that summer – but more subtly than Alex, of course.

'Yes. You followed him around the whole of that last summer we were here. Basically stalked him, if I recall.'

'He never paid me any attention.'

'Alex, you were about twelve and he must have been at least twenty. If he'd paid attention to you, he'd have been done for paedophilia. It may be Norfolk but that's still illegal.'

Perhaps he felt their eyes on him, because he stopped what he was doing and looked over. He held Cassie's eyes for a moment that lasted just a little too long, and she looked away, repulsed, suddenly, at her memories of that teenage fascination. It was a long time ago and she wasn't that girl anymore. She had grown up.

'He's looking at me,' hissed Alex. 'I'm going to go and talk to him.'

'Alex...'

But she'd already gone scampering over. Cassie watched her offer her little hand then put her head on one side and laugh in that way that had captivated so many men over the years – for a while, anyway. The guy laughed too, at whatever she was saying. He stood easily, Cassie thought, like he knew his place in the world. He'd appeared less easy in himself when he was younger, she recalled. Angrier, moodier, shoulders hunched over. But then, angry young men – they're a thing all over the world. Some of them grow out of it. Had he had any friends? Girlfriends? She couldn't remember ever seeing him with anyone, but then surely he must have done.

Great, she told herself. *That'll keep Alex busy for a bit at least.*

She turned back to the shelf and slung a bottle of vodka and some gin and wine in the basket, then went to collect the food they needed, leaving Alex to it. She'd get it done quicker that way.

They were still talking when she got to the counter. The old guy put her things through with exaggerated care. As he searched for the barcode on the vodka bottle, he said, 'What's it like living in the old place?'

'Sorry?'

'You're Lucie Maddon's nieces.'

'Did you know my aunt?'

'Everyone knew *of* your aunt, though she didn't mix much, of course. She came in here sometimes and she was always a proper lady, like they all say. Used to ask me how I was.' He smiled to himself a little and the lines around his eyes crinkled up. Then his face fell. 'Sad business all of that.'

All of that. Yes.

'We were very fond of her,' she said, wondering why a defensive note had entered her voice.

'Haven't been around these parts for years, have you?'

'No, we've been...' But she trailed off, because it was none of this guy's business what they had or hadn't been doing.

Finally, he finished putting everything through the till and she paid silently.

'Well, mind how you go,' he said.

One of those phrases that meant nothing. Cassie hated them.

'You too.' She looked across at the other side of the shop. 'Alex,' she called, 'are you ready?'

She watched her sister pat the guy on the shoulder before flitting back over to her. Cassie glanced over at him again, but he'd turned back to the shelves.

'Nice chat?'

She opened the door, pausing to hold it open for a couple of women who stared at them as they left.

'We're getting internet put in as soon as possible so we can get our food delivered instead, if they come out this far,' Cassie muttered as made their way back to the house with the bags.

Alex said nothing; she was smiling a secret smile to herself.

***

It was early that evening, when they were both sitting in the living room with drinks in their hands, that Alex said, 'Oh, by the way, I invited that guy around for a drink.'

'The guy from the shop? You invited him here?'

'Joe, his name is. Yes, why not? Is that not allowed?'

'No, it's just – oh, I don't know. We don't even bloody know him.'

'You can invite anyone you want; I don't mind. It's not my fault you've turned into some kind of hermit crab. Honestly, Cass, I'm sure you used to like having fun.'

Cassie put her hand to her head.

'Did I?'

'What is it?' Alex looked at her with narrowed eyes.

'Nothing, just a bit of—'

'Ice-pick headache?'

'Something like that.'

Joe, that was his name. *And what does it matter if he comes here?* she reasoned to herself. When all was said, he was probably dull as tarnished metal.

From somewhere up above, she heard the faint sound of scratching again. She was going to get those mice seen to before they did some real damage. Her leg twitched and she shifted impatiently in her seat.

'What is it?'

'Nothing, Alex – aren't I allowed to move?'

The memory of that little dog came back to her again and how, after it had happened, Mrs Gibbett had kept coming back here – her loyalty to Lucie, or her need to be needed, clearly surpassing everything else. She hadn't even changed in her behaviour towards Bella; or not outwardly anyway. But she couldn't have forgotten. She must have watched her, resented her...

Although, not for long, of course, because that very next winter Bella was gone and their summers by the sea ended. They said Bella drowned in the sea. They hadn't found a body, their father had told them, but they found one of her boots and that was enough. That time of year, bodies got lost – it was better not to think in too much detail about it, he'd said. When Cassie had heard, she remembered feeling frighteningly little – not even surprised – because hadn't Bella always been picking around in the sea, summer or winter, like she wanted to be a part of it? Sooner or later, she was bound to wade too far in.

But Cassie had sometimes wondered over the years whether she was really gone. Whether a person like Bella really went, or if part of them always stayed.

She looked over at Lucie's face in the photo over the piano, and slowly, there came the sensation of someone reaching around her chest and hugging, hugging. Tender at first and then harder, more insistent until she thought it would squeeze her breath away, crush her. Pushing away the rising sense of panic, she shifted again in her seat.

She became aware of a sound in her vicinity. Alex was humming Lucie's favourite song again, with that vague smile on her face.

6

It was the middle of the night and Bella was standing over the bed. She hadn't died in the sea after all, just like Cassie had suspected, and now, after all these years, she'd come back. She'd washed up and she'd come trudging out of the black waves and up the path and through the door and up the stairs... Her face in the moonlight was expressionless. That fringe she'd always refused to have trimmed fell jaggedly into her eyes, her dark hair cut to just above her shoulders. Just a child, but not a child. But then Cassie saw that Bella's face was that of a drowned person – bloated, purple, rotten, eaten-away. Cassie understood that she'd come to get her revenge, but for what? What was it? And from somewhere below, a piano was playing the *Moonlight Sonata*, the notes stealing up the stairs and into her room.

'What is it?' Cassie said, or tried to say, but her voice came out in a series of guttural, animalistic noises. Something was wrong with it; the words caught in her throat like her brain wanted them to come out but it wasn't sending the right signals. Broken synapses.

And then, right before her, Bella's face began to change. Her dry, bruised lips became full and red, and her eyes turned from pale blue to green, laughing, crinkled up at the corners. Lucie. Cassie went to reach out to her but she couldn't move her hands. Her body had gone numb. She tried to call out to her aunt to warn her, or to make her come back and help her make sense of everything.

Lucie held out her hands and she smiled, and Cassie felt reassured for a moment.

Except that when she looked down at Lucie's hands, they weren't hands at all. They were red and raw and clawed and the skin was peeling, and when she looked back up at Lucie's face, it was an empty void waiting to be filled with – what?

She woke with a gasp. Her bed, her clothes – her body – were covered in a cold sweat. Her feet were on fire and the music was still reverberating through her head like there were cold, dead fingers pressing the notes onto her brain.

She looked up, and the figure was still standing over her bed. This time, it wasn't a dream. She sat up, her heart racing.

'What the hell?'

'Cassie, you were making the weirdest noises. Like a trapped animal or something.'

Alex stood there in her pyjama shorts and vest with a deer on it, hair sleep-tousled and mascara smudges under her eyes.

'What time is it?'

'Too early to be up. I had to wake you if I wanted any fucking peace. What the hell were you dreaming about? You were making a noise like a banshee.'

Cassie stretched her legs out, flexing her toes.

'I don't remember.'

'Well, I'm going back to bed. For hours, with any luck.'

'Don't watch me sleeping again,' muttered Cassie, pulling the covers back over her.

'Just try not to do any more screaming,' said Alex, and she slammed the door behind her as she left.

Cassie closed her eyes and tried to put away the image of those clawed hands reaching out while her body burned from the feet upwards... She took in deep breaths. In for four; hold it; out for six. Slowly, slowly, the pounding in her heart eased up and she closed her eyes again. This time, thankfully, there was nothing to disturb her sleep.

***

When she woke again and looked at the time on her phone, it was close to 10 a.m. Late for her, not for Alex.

But when she got downstairs, Alex was already in the kitchen and apparently burning toast. As Cassie entered, her sister froze and pointed to her in a theatrical sort of way.

'There's something behind you...'

'Fuck off, Alex.'

'Seriously though, the noises you were making...'

'I know. You said.'

Cassie made herself a cup of tea and sat down with it at the kitchen table, taking a sip and burning her tongue a little but only half-registering the pain. She felt a jolt on her lap and looked down to see that Lucie the cat had deposited herself there. Cassie stroked her absently, still half-soaked in the memory of the dream.

'By the way,' said Alex, sitting down across from her with her burned toast and Marmite, 'do you think those mice you heard in the attic are still at it? I think I might have heard something this morning as well. Do we really want to be sharing a house with them? It's gross.'

'I only *think* it was coming from the attic.'

They both looked at each other, and then up.

'Well, *I'm* not going up there,' said Alex.

'Somebody might have to at some point. Anyway, if it's gross here, why are you staying? I can go through Lucie's things on my own.'

'Well, you haven't done much of that so far. Why should I leave, anyway? Why don't *you* leave?'

Were they actually playing some kind of chicken with the house, now? Seeing who would back down and leave first? Had it come to that?

'Anyway,' continued Alex, 'Mrs Gibbett'll find us a man to get rid of those mice, don't you worry. May as well let her be useful now she has nothing else to do around here. If it *is* mice, that is.'

'What's that supposed to mean?'

'You know, what if this place is haunted, like I said? It really wouldn't surprise me. We should have a *séance*. We could try to talk to Lucie.' Her eyes gleamed.

Cassie rolled her eyes. 'I think the only thing this place is haunted by is the past. Same as every house when it comes to that.'

'You're angry with me for some reason. What is it? Do you really hate me being here this much? Bad luck, Cass, it's my house too.'

'Oh for God's sake, Alex, I've only just got up. I just – I can't be bothered with you today, alright? I didn't sleep well. I don't want to analyse things. I want some bloody space.'

Alex stared at her for a moment, then looked down at the cat that Cassie was still stroking absently. Very deliberately, she stepped forward and picked her up.

'Don't just grab her like that, she doesn't like it.'

'You don't even like cats – what would you know about what she likes? Anyway, she's hungry. I was just about to feed her before you came in.'

Alex put the cat on the floor and clattered some food into her bowl, but, clearly put out – *And who could blame it?* thought Cassie – she scratched at the door to be let out.

'Oh, go then, Lucie,' said Alex, opening the door.

For a few seconds Alex watched the cat as she stalked off and leapt over the wall, her face working with something. Then she picked up her yoga mat and followed it, slamming the door behind her so the plates on the dresser shook and rattled.

Cassie watched her through the window as she took the path down to the beach, off to do angry yoga. Bit of an oxymoron, possibly. There was a strong summer wind today, and Alex strode through it like she was fighting it. Cassie realised she was clenching her fists, and she released them, steadying her breath.

'Sorry, Al,' she muttered.

Alone in the house, she breathed in the stillness, the only sound the ticking of Grandad Maddon's clock in the hallway. Tick-tock. Tick-tock. Always here, always here. Then she felt it again: the prickling that worked its way up her spine to the back of her neck and down into her hands. When she looked at them, they were clenched and red. She stood up with a jerk, pushing herself away from the table, and before she could consider what she was really doing, she went to the cupboard in the sitting room, where she took a swig from the bottle of gin to ward away the feeling, or at least banish it to the background, before marching resolutely up the stairs.

Who's afraid of the big, bad attic? Who's afraid of Grandad Maddon? Not me.

At the top of the stairs, she paused to look out of the tall window, over the garden and the cliff and the beach beyond it; Alex was on the sand, in downward dog.

Is it this place? Does it send people mad? Does it make their brains fall away bit by bit like the cliffs?

The doctors don't know for sure, but these things – these ailments – can sometimes be environmental.

Who's afraid of Cousin Bella?

Who's afraid but doesn't know what they're afraid of?

Who's afraid of themselves?

Stop it, she told herself.

Alex was saluting the sun now. And it had been a day just like this one on the beach, with the crab, all those years ago. All summer long and the whole place – the whole expanse of Norfolk sands from here to the pier – had been hers and Alex's for the most part. No holidaymakers walked this far – there were no chip shops, no cafés or arcades on this bit of the shore – just the few people from the houses nearby walking their dogs or whatever it was they did to pass the time.

The sun had poured itself onto them that day. If she tried, she could still feel the burning on her shoulders, the pressure in the top of her head. Just like today, it wasn't *good* sun; there was something relentless about it, and the sea had still been grey, not blue like the Mediterranean. The house on the cliff had towered over them, and looking up at it was dizzying. If you lay on your back on the sand, the roof seemed to rotate slowly, like it was about to fall and crush all the life out of your body.

That day, they'd been idly building a giant sandcastle, with a moat: at fourteen and twelve, too old to really put their all into it, not old enough to give up playing in favour of sunbathing. Alex in a striped sundress, Cassie in jeans and a T-shirt. They were happy enough in each other's company then, but of course, that day there'd been someone else with them, too – the little daughter of the woman who used to come and clean the house for Lucie. In what Cassie would come to think of as some kind of weird semi-feudal throwback that only existed out in places like this, the mother would never speak to them as she worked – never even meet their eyes – but the girl had been a sweet little thing with red hair, only five or six, and they hadn't minded having her with them. She clearly didn't like being in the cliff house – said it frightened her and there were 'bad' things in there, but then kids could be fanciful – so instead she followed them around like a little familiar. Sometimes she asked odd, disconcerting questions, like *why does your auntie not smile when she's on her own?* Or *what is your cousin angry for all the time?* But still, they'd been content that day, in their way, the three of them, the girl singing ring-a-ring of roses to herself and occasionally falling down.

Except then Bella had appeared. Usually, she stayed away from them, and they were glad about that because they didn't want her pale, unsettling eyes on them hour after hour. That day, however, she'd emerged out of the sea like something inhuman, with her hands red-raw from that constant scratching and plunging in the cold saltwater. They'd been digging a moat to go around the castle. When Bella reached them, she sat on a mound of sand, occasionally biting idly at her hands and watching them dig but making no move to join in – it was like she was waiting for something.

A movement in the sand, between them; a large crab crawled out of a hole and did its funny sideways scuttle towards them. The little girl stopped and laughed at it, her pale face lit up, and Cassie and Alex laughed too, more at her laughing than anything else, probably.

Then Bella reached down from her throne of sand and picked the crab up between two fingers. The thing wriggled there, its claws moving in and out. Alex gave a little shriek of disgust.

'Put it down!'

Very slowly and deliberately, Bella put her fingers on either side of the wriggling crab and *ripped it apart*. Cassie watched the parts of it fall to pieces, and there was an awful cracking sound. But she could do nothing, and as she looked at the other two, she saw their mouths were open, as hers must have been.

Then she moved forward and knocked the creature out of Bella's hands.

'Don't, Bella. Stop.' But it was too late by then, of course.

Bella looked at her, and for the first time, she registered an expression. It was a kind of perplexed triumph that was so strange she still recalled it perfectly all these years later. Cassie had looked away from her cousin and down at the mutilated crab on the sand. Its claws were beautiful, she saw: red and blue and dotted here and there with little speckles of white. She wanted to retch.

And Cassie remembered how she'd suddenly looked up at the house, and her aunt had been standing in the tall window at the top of the stairs – where she herself was standing right now, years later. Lucie couldn't have seen what had happened from all that way, of course – how could she? She'd put her arm up as if to wave at her aunt, and then put it down again.

The little girl had begun to cry. She'd wanted to bury the crab in the sand, and they'd had to explain to her that the sea would just wash it up again. She'd held her doll to her – a battered old object with glassy, pale blue eyes that she always carried with her and sometimes pretended to feed, like insipid little Beth March.

Cassie shook her head, trying to dispel the long-ago image of that twitching crab, of Bella, of the little girl. She turned away from the window and forced her legs along the landing to the door that led to the attic. The one she'd been avoiding ever since they got here because of... But why should she? It was just a room, that was all, and dammit she was going to find those mice.

She turned the door handle and pulled, but it wouldn't open at first. She flexed her fingers and wrapped them around it again, pulling harder, harder, and suddenly the door to the stairs flew open with a force that almost sent her flying backwards.

She reached in and gripped the banister to steady herself – who knew how stable these stairs were? – and ascended into darkness. She remembered there was a light switch at the top, but when she tried it nothing happened. She should have brought a torch, but she wasn't even sure such a thing existed in Lucie's house.

Oh God, that smell – what was it? It was like the sea, but rotten. And she was breathing in something, too. Something like dust but thicker and more cloying and more – more *alive*, somehow. *Can dust be alive?*

Had something scuttled into the corner? She remembered her phone in her pocket, took it out and switched it on so it emitted a feeble blueish glow. She shone it over to where the sound had come from, but if there had been anything, it had hidden now. She pointed it up to the beams and saw they were uneven, jagged, like scars across the roof of the attic.

This had always been Bella's territory; it was where she'd come – from *choice* – to be alone. There was a single wooden chair in the corner and a cushion on the floor but no other sign of anything designed for human comfort. Cassie's eyes were getting more used to the dark now, and she could see that, next to the cushion, there was a plain wooden box with a lid. Somehow she knew that the smell and the scratching were both coming from near there.

She'd only been up here once before, and that was because she'd lost some stupid bet with Alex so she'd had to take a dare and, well, she'd perhaps had a sense of honour back then. She'd only been in there a few moments and she'd been about to prise open the lid of the box – out of curiosity, she supposed – before Bella came. She remembered the look on Bella's face when it had appeared at the top of the stairs. Rage, mixed with something like fear. Like she'd been *violated* in some way. Cassie had tried to calm her down, and Bella had reached over and pushed the lid shut, catching it on one of Cassie's fingers so she let out a cry (she still had the scar from that day on her fingertip).

'I'm sorry, Bella,' she'd tried to say. 'But you don't have to be so—'

And Bella had lunged at her with those red-raw claws of hers and they'd fastened around her neck before she knew what was happening, and there was real hate in her cousin's eyes then. She was so strong – that's what Cassie remembered most. But somehow Cassie had managed to push her away and she'd half-run, half-fallen down the stairs and tried to open the door, only Alex – fucking Alex – had turned the key in the lock, and Cassie could hear her giggling wildly on the outside. She banged on the door to be let out, because at that moment she'd genuinely thought Bella was going to kill her. Finally, Lucie had come, and it was the only time Cassie had ever seen her looking annoyed with her or Alex. And again, there was something in the way she'd looked at Bella then – something that hadn't been Lucie at all.

The scratching had stopped, just like that. Like she was outside – beyond – herself now, she edged forward in the dim blue phone light and slowly opened the lid, touching it with the tips of her fingers only. She braced herself for something small and furry to scuttle out; to leap at her, even.

The smell flew out and up her nose and down her throat and even in her eyes so for a moment she could hardly see. She put her hand over her mouth and held her phone over the objects inside the box.

Crab claws, dozens of them – all different kinds and sizes. A charnel house for crustaceans. Bella's prized possessions. She saw her hand – suddenly numb and not a part of her, like she'd been sleeping on it – reach out to pick one up of the claws, one of the bigger ones. It was red and blue and white, like the one on the beach that day.

But as she picked it up, it crumbled to dust in her hands and she heard a sound. It was something between a hiss and a sigh, and it seemed to come from all around her.

Cassie was not afraid – she was beyond fear these days, she told herself – but still she slammed the lid of the box and made her way back to the top of the stairs. Except when she got there, she felt that tight band around her chest again, as though something was holding her fast and soon she would be unable to breathe. She dropped her phone and it clattered to the bottom of the stairs, and then she was in darkness.

And somewhere downstairs, beyond the attic door and in the real world of the present, Lucie the cat was miaowing like she wanted her to come out. (*'Alex, it's not funny; unlock the door.'*) Fighting the dizzy sensation in her head, she began to work her way down the stairs towards the sound like an audible lighthouse (*soundhouse?*), but somehow her legs had seized up, like matchsticks. She was a brittle matchstick doll, or a rusty pair of scissors that couldn't even cut paper anymore.

Half falling, half crawling in the darkness, she made it to the foot of the stairs and grasped the wall to steady herself. Then she felt a sharp pain across her left palm, like something had bitten her. She realised there was something sticking out of the wall — a nail, a jagged piece of wood? The throbbing was acute, but the suddenness of it had the effect, somehow, of taking her away from the other things, of bringing her back to herself, the way you dig your fingernails into your palm when they're taking blood from you for the thousandth time, and suddenly you can't feel the needle going in. Instinctively, she put her hand to her mouth and tasted blood, and then drew it away because there would be other things, too: decades of dirt and decay.

The cat was miaowing still and scratching at the door, and she felt — she was certain of it — a cold breath on her neck. She didn't wait to look around her; she pushed the door open and stumbled out into the light, almost tripping over Lucie.

You bloody idiot, she said to herself now, standing for a moment to steady her breath, feeling foolish in the full glare of the sunlight coming in through the big window at the end of the landing.

She examined her hand and was annoyed to see a nasty, untidy gash across the palm. Blood mixed with dust and grime. The bathroom was directly next to the attic stairs, so she went in and began to clean her hand with soap, almost luxuriating in the bright, human sting. Once she was done, she came out again and stood looking at the attic door. She realised then that she was shaking.

Don't be a twat, Cassie. You're not the kind of person to let this sort of thing rattle you.

There was a loud smash from downstairs, like something had been thrown violently to the floor. The cat leapt away from her, eyes big and startled, and disappeared around the bathroom door.

7

When Cassie reached the top of the stairs, she saw Alex in the hallway gaping after the cat as it made its wild dash out towards the kitchen.

'What was that crash? Did you break something?'

'I don't know what it was,' said Alex, eyes looking innocently up at her, her anger from earlier apparently forgotten. 'I've just come in from the beach. I think it came from the living room.'

She waited for Cassie to reach the bottom of the staircase, and the two of them went into the room together. It was obvious in a second what had happened: the framed photo of the two of them and Lucie, with Bella in the background, the one that had been on top of the piano, lay smashed on the floor, almost like it had been thrown, violently. But that was not the worst thing. Somehow, the urn holding Lucie's ashes had also fallen from its place on the high shelf. The lid was off and there were ashes all over the floor. There were ashes in the *air*. Next to it, the French windows were wide open.

'No!' said Alex. She ran towards the mess and began, crazily, to try to catch some of the floating ashes and for a moment Cassie was reminded of watching Alex at a birthday party when they'd been small children, trying to catch bubbles. 'Why did you leave the window open with this wind blowing?'

'Don't blame me for this. Watch it! There's broken glass on the floor and you're not wearing anything on your feet.' Very big sister, all of a sudden. 'And it wasn't me that left it open.'

Cassie stepped forward, holding her damaged hand against her so Alex couldn't see, her thick socks protecting her – she imagined – against any shards of glass. She picked up the shattered frame and removed the photo gently, stroking Lucie's face without realising she was doing it. Then she saw Alex watching her, so she placed the photo up on the sideboard. She bent down again and picked up the urn, still intact, and tried to scrape some of the ashes back in, but they were mixed with the dust on the floorboards (they hadn't exactly been keeping the place clean, it turned out, any more than they'd been sorting through Lucie's things like they were supposed to). She bowed her head in a rush of pointless grief.

There was a tap at the kitchen door.

'It'll be Mrs Gibbett again,' said Alex. 'Can't we have a break from her for one day?'

'I'll get it,' said Cassie. 'If it's Mrs Gibbett, I'll get rid of her.' She left Alex kneeling in the ashes and wiping her eyes.

But it wasn't Mrs Gibbett. When she opened the door, it was the guy from the shop the other day. Up close he was tanned, healthy-looking, like he ate his five-a-day or even more. She felt suddenly self-conscious. She was so pale, so thin and possibly sickly-looking, in comparison. He had bright blue eyes, she noticed, a little close-set but not unattractively so. There were lines around the corners of them, and they crinkled up now as he smiled at her.

'Hello?' she said.

'Sorry to disturb you. I'm Joe. You must be – Cassie, right?'

'That's right.'

'I was just walking to the beach but I remembered – the other day, Alex, your sister, said to come over if I felt like it. Tell you the truth, I don't really know anyone around here anymore so I thought it might be nice... while I'm here.'

Then why come back here at all? He might have asked her the same question, she supposed. But at least she and Alex had a reason, of sorts.

'Yes, she told me. Nice to meet you, Joe.'

Unlike her, the guy wasn't in the least bit uneasy. He stood square, looking her straight in the eye. She pushed a lock of hair from her face, trying to remember the last time she'd had it cut or the last time she'd worn makeup. She realised, suddenly, she'd been living like someone who didn't expect to speak to other people for a long time, if ever again. Was it her choice? Back in London, once upon a time, she'd been someone who saw people and went to parties now and then and went to museums and – well, *did things*, for Christ's sake. She'd even had an oh-so-nice-and-eligible boyfriend not so long ago, even if she'd long since tired of him.

(*'That's right – push me away like you do everyone else. You think you don't need people Cassie, but right now you...'*)

'Joe, you came!'

Alex edged in beside her, suddenly much brighter again. Cassie had never ceased to marvel at the way her mood could turn from moment to moment.

'Invite him in then, Cassie.' She shook her head and turned to Joe. 'She's only been here for a couple of weeks and she's forgotten how normal people behave.'

'Aren't you normal people?' His eyes were slightly teasing.

'Well, you know... Anyway, come through and see the remnants of the explosion.' She grabbed his hand and pulled him into the kitchen. No sense of personal space, but the guy didn't seem to mind.

Cassie followed after them.

'What's gone on in here?' he said, looking at the glass on the floor of the living room.

'We're under attack,' said Alex. She had her hand on his arm and she hadn't let go of it yet.

'I can see.'

Cassie watched him as he picked up the picture she'd put down on the sideboard and looked at it just a fraction longer than necessary.

'Attractive, weren't we?' said Alex.

'Are you sure you haven't just been throwing things at each other?'

'Not yet,' said Alex, looking at Cassie meaningfully.

During all this, Cassie had been holding her cut hand to her to stop them from seeing that she was bleeding, but either the guy had sharp eyes or he could smell blood.

'You've hurt yourself,' he said.

Alex looked at her now. 'Bloody hell, Cass, yes – did you cut it on the glass or something? You're going to bleed all over everything. And you were telling *me* to be careful.'

'It'll stop soon.'

'Can I see? You might need stitches if it's bad,' said the guy. 'I know a bit about that sort of thing.'

Cassie held her hand closer to herself. She knew the blood was seeping through the cloth she'd wrapped around it.

'It's fine. I think there are bandages around here some-where.'

Alex was losing interest.

'Well, go and grab some then, before this really does start to look like a crime scene. So, what brings you here?' she said, turning to face Joe and putting her head on one side.

Alex had made him her new mission; Cassie could see that already. She'd relive all her youthful fantasies on this childhood crush, like she'd done with every man she'd met in the years since she'd left home – and there'd been plenty of them – until it blew up in her face like it always did. Be-cause none of them – not this guy, or the one who owned a yacht or the one who ran a pub and dealt crack on the side – were going to make up for what she lacked. What they both lacked.

Suddenly, Cassie wanted to scream at the sheer predict-able inevitability of everything. Life, she thought sudden-ly, was like being in a car and careening into a wall at top speed, only you couldn't stop; you could never stop. Her head was pounding, and the world around her began to go dim. *Don't let them see.*

'Hello?'

The voice came from the still-open kitchen door.

'Oh God, it's her,' said Cassie. 'Quick, into the kitchen before she sees all this and makes a God-almighty fuss.'

The woman was standing expectantly in the doorway as the three of them trooped in. Her face changed a little when she saw Joe. Her lips – what there was of them – pursed.

Probably thinks he's going to take advantage of us two innocent young girls.

'Oh, I didn't realise you had a guest. I've just brought you some potatoes.'

She waved a netted bag at them, and it sprinkled dried dirt onto the floor.

'This is Joe,' said Alex. 'But I expect you must know that already.'

'Yes – yes, I know. Hello, Joseph, it must have been years since you've been back here. Not since your poor mum and dad went.'

'I know, it's been a long time.' He smiled at her, but it seemed forced now, and he immediately turned to face Alex. 'I only popped round on the off chance to see if either of you two want to join me for a walk along the beach?' he said.

Mrs Gibbett looked from one to the other.

'Lovely to have all this free time. Well, I won't keep you – I don't want to be in the way. I'll put these here. See you soon, girls.'

'Yes, see you.'

She deposited the bag on the table and hurried out of the door.

Alex turned to Joe with a grimace. 'That's the quickest we've managed to get rid of her since we arrived here. You'll have to tell me your secret. Anyway, I'd *love* a walk.' She looked at Cassie, as if daring her to come too.

'Thanks for the invite, but I'll stay here and cauterise the wound and clear up this mess. Nice to meet you, Joe. Again, I mean,' she said, turning away from his eyes. Her fingers were going cold; she couldn't hold on much longer.

'You too, Cassie. See you soon.'

'Don't bleed to death,' added Alex.

They headed down the path through the sand dunes. She watched them for a moment until they were out of sight, breathing heavily, and then she rushed over to the kitchen sink, put her head over it and vomited. When she was done, she sank down onto a kitchen chair, put her head on her arms and focused hard on the throbbing in her hand, the arterial beat (like the baby's heartbeat she'd heard that time, but she'd seen to *that*, he'd asked her not to but how could she...).

Tick-tock. Tick-tock. Ba-boom. Ba-boom.

8

It had taken her a while to find the grave in the sprawling churchyard. In fact, she'd begun to wonder if it even existed.

The church was set on the edge of the town with a long graveyard that stretched on and on. It was cooler here, at least; in the time-honoured tradition of graveyards, it was coming down with willows and they cast a bit of shade. The church itself must have been a pretty building once but now it looked in danger of imminent collapse. The roof, as Mrs Gibbett was so fond of telling them, was in desperate need of repair. There was scaffolding around it but no construction workers to be seen.

She found it in the end. Just a small marker, not a huge headstone like some of the others, unremarkable in itself. The graves around it were well taken care of. Some had little vases of flowers or ornaments or even, in one case, a spinning toy windmill, but this one was surrounded with weeds and there was some kind of ugly dark fungus. She crouched down for a moment. Should she have brought flowers, she wondered now. You were supposed to bring lilies for the dead, weren't you? But then, maybe not *this* particular dead. This one probably didn't deserve it. She wasn't even sure why she had come here today, except that she'd felt the need to leave the house, so she'd come into town and this was where her feet had taken her, apparently independently of herself.

She stood up again, awkwardly, her legs protesting, trying not to overbalance and fall face-first into a headstone. Before she left, she glanced back once more at Grandad

Maddon's miserable grave. She'd never known him, but suddenly she wanted to tell him that it was all his fault; that it was because of him, somehow, that Lucie was no longer here; that she and Alex had no mother and no aunt. And then she noticed something. Some words or markings someone had gouged into it. She bent closer to have a look.

In Hell, it said.

***

Hurrying back through the centre of the town, Cassie was confronted with signs wherever she looked: '*Summer Fete*'. '*See the Carnival Queen crowned*'. '*Book your place at the craft fayre*'. Another one with a picture of a child, asking her, '*Are you a safe speed driver?*' Something that looked suspiciously like a gallows was being erected in the town square, but she imagined it must be something to do with the aforementioned Carnival Queen.

She hadn't been into town since she'd arrived at the house, but her first impression was that it had barely changed from when she'd been a child. As she'd observed on her drive through here a few weeks ago, it was the same collection of pubs, antique shops, chip shops, second-hand bookshops, cafés and all the other kinds of things that make up the life of a small coastal town. There was little sign of bustle on a late Wednesday morning. She looked in the window of a secondhand shop on the high street and her heart stopped.

Lucie?

For a second she saw her, standing there, until she realised: it was just a mannequin. A mannequin with dark hair and red lips and wearing a wide-skirted dress pulled in at the waist.

Then she saw them, across the street, just next to the war memorial in the town centre: Alex and Joe. And she'd come away from the house on purpose to avoid them. Instinctively, she ducked into an alleyway that led down to the car park and peered out at them. Her sister was got up in the floaty summer dress she'd put on that morning, cut artfully to cling to her in the right places. She'd teamed this with an oversized floppy hat and some jewelled sandals. She looked like she was going to a boho wedding.

Alex had her arm linked through Joe's and she was laughing; Cassie could hear her from across the street. She waited and watched them as they went into the pub across from the market square. She hadn't realised she'd been holding her breath until the door closed behind them and their laughter.

'Excuse me?'

She turned. An elderly man and woman were standing in front of her. They looked unnervingly eager, like chickens with beady eyes waiting for scraps.

'Hello?'

'We just wanted to – that is, you're Lucie Maddon's niece, aren't you?' said the woman. 'We saw you the other day in the shop and we wanted to say hello but we weren't sure...'

'Yes, that's right.'

Would they sense that Cassie had no time, no energy for small talk?

'We just wanted to say it's nice to see you in these parts.' She reached out with an arthritic hand to touch Cassie's arm. 'It's lovely that you're here. Everyone liked your aunt, you know.'

No mention of Bella – there never was.

Cassie drew herself away from the clutching hand. 'Well, thank you...'

'Lovely woman, your aunt was. Wonderful. Everyone said so...'

Wherever she went, Lucie was everywhere and the whole place – the house, the beach, the town – still felt the absence of her. This was how it was going to be, on and on into the future. As long as she lived.

Minutes later, she sat in a café with a decaf latte and wished it was something stronger. She could see, in fact, that there was wine behind the counter, but might it be a little early for that, even by her standards? In any case, she had to drive back and she had to be a safe speed driver as the sign had instructed her.

Alex and Joe; Joe and Alex – laughing together right now in the pub with not a care in the world. She thought back to the only time Joe had spoken to her when she was a child – not that he would remember it, she supposed. She'd been fourteen, that particular summer, but she'd looked older, or felt older. She'd been sitting out on a rock a little way along the beach, watching the seagulls circling, and she hadn't even realised she'd been crying until she heard the voice.

'Are you OK there? You're from the big house, aren't you?'

She'd looked up and there he was – an actual, grown-up man – looking down at her, and she felt her heart skip a little and she thought, *Is this what it's like when you're beginning not to be a child anymore?* He was accompanied by a big, shaggy dog that was leaping up at him, clearly eager to be moving on.

(Just that morning, she'd started bleeding for the first time. Lucie'd found her a pad, showed her what to do with it, and she was somehow shamefully conscious of the blood as she sat there, looking up at him.)

She sniffed and wiped her eyes. She was angry, but not at him.

'I'm fine, it's nothing.' Control, always control. Cassie needed nobody's help or sympathy.

Her father had rung that morning to say he was taking wife number three away to Europe for a few months – maybe till Christmas – so that was that. It wasn't a surprise exactly, and normally Cassie wouldn't care, but that day it had made her – bitter. And it had made Alex cry, too. She'd run upstairs to her room and slammed the door, and they hadn't seen her since. Back then, as now, she'd felt exhaustingly protective of her little sister and her terrible, performative sensitivity.

He'd smiled at her and for a moment it was the most astonishing thing she had ever seen. She wanted him to keep smiling at her like that; she wanted him to sit down and put his arm around her narrow shoulders, but instead, she simply froze and stared up at him. He must have thought she had something wrong with her, like Bella.

'Well, I'm probably disturbing you and you want to be alone – big ignorant bloke stepping on your space. Don't stay out here too long, love; the tide's coming in.'

He carried on walking further up the beach, apparently not heeding his own warning about the tide, and she wanted to follow him, but instead, she just watched him go and tried to ignore the gnawing ache in her belly.

She'd never told Alex about this, because there was nothing to tell – or at least nothing that anybody else would have understood. But she'd always remembered that day because it had changed something in her. No one since had produced that spark of elation – that kind of awakening – she'd felt at that moment. Funny.

And now here she was, in her late thirties and sitting by herself in a café daydreaming like a crazed spinster. One drink wouldn't hurt, if she ordered some food, too. To hell with what any of these people thought. She went up to the counter and ordered a tuna salad and a glass of Sauvignon Blanc – medium, as a compromise. When she sat back down at her table away from the window, she saw that a young family had come in: mum, dad and a little girl playing around the table near their feet. They looked tired but happy, in a way she couldn't comprehend.

The dad kissed the mum and went over to the counter to make their order. The little girl refused to sit on the chair offered to her; instead, she began to explore the room on sturdy, determined little legs. She went up to the other customers one by one, gazing at them quizzically. They all smiled benignly at her or said things like, 'What a confident little girl' or 'Look at those big blue eyes.' Cassie knew the girl would come up to her in a moment and she would have to arrange her face in an acceptable manner. And sure enough, the child stopped in front of her and *looked* at her, thoughtfully. She felt a reflexive downwards tugging, somewhere around her midsection, as though something was being ripped out of her.

Didn't anyone tell you it's bloody rude to stare?

Someone – probably the mother – had spent ages and ages putting the girl's hair into an intricate French braid.

There'd never been any of that for her and Alex when they were growing up.

'Poppy!' The mum laughed from across the room. 'Stop bothering people.'

But she didn't say it seriously. *'How could anyone possibly be bothered by my darling child?'* said her eyes.

The child continued to stare and then she held out her hand. Cassie looked across the room at the mother, and their eyes met for a moment.

She's thinking, 'Look at the woman drinking alone'.

The woman's fond smile left her face then, and she came over and picked her daughter up.

'Sorry,' she said to Cassie and then a 'Come on, trouble,' to the daughter.

The dad had come back from the counter with a carton of juice, and this time the girl sat happily preoccupied on her chair.

The other people in the café – the two elderly ladies and the guy with his newspaper –were staring at Cassie now as though there was something wrong with her, or she'd done something unacceptable. She finished her wine, pushed aside her half-eaten salad and walked out. On the way back to the car, on a whim, she stopped at a florist's to buy some lilies. Mourning flowers for Lucie, and maybe even for Bella, too. Better late than never, as they say.

As she left town, she found she was driving directly into the sun and pulling the visor down over the windscreen made no difference at all. Couldn't see. Couldn't see the road.

But something else was happening to her eyes, too. Her vision was starting to split in the most disorientating way, like the world was turning into a kaleidoscope and maybe it had always been and she was only seeing it now for the first time. She needed to pull over; perhaps it had been too early for that glass of wine, after all. Her wounded hand, which stubbornly refused to heal, was throbbing.

And right then she saw the figure in front of her, and she slammed on the brakes and swerved to the side of the road, coming to a skidding halt on the verge. She sat there, shaking.

Oh Christ, had she been weaving over the road? Had she hurt someone? *Killed* them? She'd be arrested and Alex would love that, was her first thought – Cassie in trouble for once.

She pulled herself together and opened the car door, her vision starting to come back into focus.

She'd come to a stop in a kind of dip in the road next to a hedge, and her aunt's house was still a mile or so up ahead. There was no pavement, but a path had been beaten alongside the hedge, and it was here she saw the woman with the baby who'd been at the bus stop the other day, only this time the baby was in a pram. The woman stared at her without speaking, and for a moment Cassie stared back, before realising it was really up to her to break this silence as she'd nearly mown them both down. *Sweet Jesus.*

She pushed open the car door and hurried over to her. Yes, it was definitely her, just as she'd thought: their little beach playmate with the red hair from all those years back, but older, of course, and now with that livid scar down the side of her face.

'Oh God, I'm so sorry – the sun got in my eyes. I nearly hit you and your – your baby. Are you hurt? Is the...'

Except what were you doing in the middle of the fucking road?

The woman continued to stare at Cassie without blinking. Was there something *wrong* with her, or was she possibly even in some kind of shock? Cassie glanced uneasily towards the pram; there was no sound coming from it at all. She was no expert, but weren't babies supposed to cry or gurgle or – something?

'Billie, that's your name, isn't it? Do you remember me? From years ago? You used to come along with me and my sister Alex sometimes, remember? How is your mother?'

Finally, the woman said, 'You didn't nearly hit me.'

'But you were on the road when I came round the corner. I...'

She shook her head. 'I was just standing right here and you pulled over quick like you'd got scared of something. Are you scared?'

Cassie's legs felt wobbly. Maybe *she* was the one in shock. She sat back on the car bonnet and looked at the woman with the pram.

'But you're sure you're OK?'

'I'm fine.'

'You're sure? Look, maybe I should take you...'

'No.'

'Is it safe – you know – walking down this road with a pram? That's not much of a path.'

'Yes, it's safe.' And then: 'I remember you. Bella was your cousin.'

'That's right.'

She must have been the first person since they'd got here to acknowledge Bella had even been alive. Her face was solemn; as a small girl she'd laughed all the time. She'd had eyes that had sparkled. The years had changed her. Or maybe this was how she'd been since...

But now the woman did smile: only a tentative tugging at the corners of her mouth, but for a second it transformed her face. Hard to think of her as a woman, in fact, when the last time she'd seen her she'd been a six-year-old child. How could she be a mother? Probably one of those depressing tales you heard of a naïve local girl taken advantage of... She shook the thought away. This wasn't a Thomas Hardy novel.

'Would you like a lift back in the car?' Cassie asked.

Like she'd want to get in a car with you now.

'No, I always walk.'

'And you're sure – you're sure the baby is OK?'

Suddenly, Cassie had to see – make sure it wasn't damaged or upset in some way, or however babies got. It was still so terribly silent.

'Do you mind?'

She stepped over and peered into the pram under the blankets, preparing the face that people expected when you looked at their babies.

But in the pram there was just an old-fashioned doll with matted dark hair, cold blue eyes with a few remaining lashes stuck to the lids. Some kind of bug was making its way into one of them. Dirty face. Cracked face.

'Oh, I'm...' She looked up at Billie, lost for words, and Billie looked back at her.

'She's bad,' said Billie.

'Who?'

'In the house.'

'Bella?' Cassie's voice was soft now. 'Are you talking about my cousin Bella? I remember what happened that day – but she's gone, you know.'

Just then, another car came speeding around the corner and honked its horn at them.

Cassie turned briefly to shout 'Arsehole!' after it, and the small expression of anger made her feel better. Then she turned back to Billie, but somehow, in that brief period of time, she had already tucked the blanket back around the baby doll and walked off in the direction of town. Cassie watched the retreating figure until she was out of sight, but she never went after her.

***

By the time Cassie got back to the house, she felt dirty like that tattered old doll. Maybe it was the sticky heat, maybe it was something else, but whatever the cause, there was an itching, prickling feeling all over her skin. Alex was not back yet, so she dumped the impulse-bought lilies hastily in one of Lucie's vases on the windowsill, poured herself a glass of wine from the fridge and went straight upstairs into the bathroom with the clawed-foot tub. She'd always enjoyed being in this bath when she was a kid because she'd imagined it was a friendly monster waiting to take her into a warm embrace. Lucie always told her she had a great imagination.

She put her uninjured hand underneath the running water and felt it burning, getting hotter and hotter, but she didn't take it away at first. She wanted to see how long she could hold it there before the pain got too much. She thought of the woman with the doll and the pram again. Little Billie. Sweet child. She remembered Billie's tears as she'd buried that broken crab in the sand.

The sound of the running water was loud in the large, high-ceilinged room. Fancy bathroom – the kind that people aspire to. Only now, the windows were edged with toxic black mould and beyond the door there was the attic with its scratch, scratch, scratch.

She slipped off her clothes into a pile on the floor and climbed in, revelling in the heat, feeling the steam reddening her face and her lips. Breathing it in. *She* was still alive, whatever that meant. She picked up the glass of wine from the windowsill where she'd placed it, drained half and then sank into the water.

She was alive, yes, but she didn't have to be. She played with the idea in her mind like a new and interesting toy. Really, it was an intellectual proposition, this ability to choose how much you want to engage with life and how much you are willing to accept. Can you divorce it from feeling? Emotion? Make it a practical transaction with yourself? Cassie was no deluded fool; she knew she was privileged, whatever that meant. She would not tell herself that nobody would miss her – she did not indulge in self-pity. Some would miss her, some wouldn't. Everyone would get on with their lives all the same. That was how it happened.

From somewhere far, far below, in another place, she heard the slam of a door and muffled voices.

'Cassie?'

'In the bath,' she called down. Her voice sounded raspy, echoey in here.

The point was that she, Cassie, was in control. She was so in control that she could choose when she lived and when she died. Not like other people.

She leaned back, back, into the claw-foot monster, and closed her eyes.

'Where's the ice?' came Alex's muffled voice again.

'Try the freezer,' she shouted back.

She leant back further still until everything was underwater but the tip of her nose. She could go down a little further, if she wanted. But would your body fight it? Would it know what you were trying to do and push itself up for air? Then, for a moment, another flash of – what, memory? Hallucination?

Opening the door by accident and Bella's sitting in the bath, skinny and obscenely pale apart from those peeled, red-raw hands. Lucie's standing over her with her arms wrapped around her waist – physically holding herself to-gether – then their faces both snap towards you and you can feel your face getting redder as you apologise and beat a hasty, appalled retreat and you try not to look at Bella there in the bath with the ugly marks on her body...

She could hear a muffled sound like footsteps going up and down stairs, and then faint laughter, but all distorted by the water in her ears so it sounded far away. And then there was the soft, sonorous drone of music.

And something else was happening, something unexpected. She was no longer the one holding her face under the water. There was something else, something pushing her downwards. The someone, the something, that had been trying to crush her ribs these past few weeks, held her in an oppressive, hateful embrace and forced her down. She tried to open her eyes, but the water flooded in and she realised that her control had only ever been an illusion. Then, clear as anything, a low, harsh voice inside her head that was hers but not hers:

'You'll never be clean. Never.'

Downstairs, Alex had put music on. Cassie could hear the sonorous moan from beyond the prison of the water, the way that music would sound in a dream. Laughter again, dry and mirthless, but this time it was closer, as though it was coming from somewhere in the room or somewhere inside her head. For the first time in a long time, real fear set in. There was something or someone trying to take control of her body. It had been trying for months now and maybe it was finally going to have its way. The choice wasn't hers anymore but they'd all say...

Laughter again, and then, clearer and closer, the scratching again, urgent now. With a sudden rush of something –

was it defiance? – she pushed herself up and she was back in the room and the sound of the music and the world around her became real and she was drawing in the air around her in big, choking gulps.

Not this time.

She looked across and the door was standing wide open. Lucie the cat was sitting on the bathroom floor, looking up at her anxiously, if cats could look anxious.

'Was that you making all that noise?' she gasped, as her breathing subsided. 'Can you open doors now?'

Lucie blinked. Cassie took another deep breath and sank backwards again. Somehow, there were beads of sweat on her forehead.

Alex could walk in, and whoever was with her – Joe, presumably – could walk in, too. They'd see her lying in here, pink and stretched and naked, and they wouldn't know that just seconds ago she'd been fighting for breath.

It was fine. It was all fine. It was all nothing. She put her good hand on the side of the tub and pulled herself up. For a moment, the world span as the blood rushed to her head, and then mercifully righted itself.

9

Standing at the foot of the stairs, next to the ticking clock, she could hear voices from the kitchen. She wondered what Joe and Alex found to talk about together, what new things they were discovering about each other in that dance that people did when they were at the start of something. Instead of going to join them, she turned left into the sitting room, opening the French windows and standing half-in, half-out to let the early evening breeze play around her wet hair and down her bare arms, still flecked with droplets of bathwater. Cassie had put a fresh dressing on her hand, but the faint throbbing, like an aching pulse, remained. She could hear the sea from here: the now-familiar sound of gulls crying out and a horn, or something, from a faraway ship. There was something sad about being by the sea in the evening. She frowned, gripping the side of her left arm with her fingers.

'Are you OK?'

She spun around to see Joe standing behind her, a little closer than was comfortable. She could smell him: musky, some kind of aftershave – not cheap, not expensive either. There were fair hairs on his arms, running down on either side of that alligator scar. Up close, his face was stubbled, faintly pockmarked, and he had lines around his eyes now as he smiled at her in an apologetic sort of way. She drew back slightly, oddly repulsed.

'I didn't hear you come in.'

The way he was looking at her, she almost felt he could see on her face something of what had passed that day, so she closed it up, deliberately, like a box. She'd taught herself how to do that long ago. Back when she was a teenager and they'd sent her away to that place for a while and they'd all asked her questions and tried to pry into her head, even though she'd known she was cleverer than them all. White coats and concerned faces and other young people sitting around pale and bewildered and trapped...

But he was talking to her.

'... didn't mean to startle you. Alex made me some pasta – have you eaten? There's some left.'

'It's alright, I'm not hungry – it's too hot.'

He nodded to the garden.

'It's looking pretty wild out there. Wasn't like that years ago when Dad took care of it.'

'That's right, I forgot; your dad looked after the garden, didn't he? You used to come and help him sometimes.'

Of course she hadn't forgotten. Alex's eager face peering out the window as he worked in the hot sun. *He's taking his top off, Cassie – come and see.'* Her feigning disinterest; she *would not* look in front of Alex.

'I was sorry to hear about your aunt.'

'Oh. Did you know Lucie well at all?'

He paused for a moment, still looking out of the French windows as if deciding what to say.

'I don't think anyone around here really knew her well, but you realised that, right? She was... private, everyone said.' He shrugged. 'I could understand that. She was a nice lady – always nice to me and Dad, anyway.'

'Al and I loved her – a bit too much, I think. We didn't really have much of a home base; we were either at boarding school or moving around for Dad's work, so I guess this was stability for us, in a way, coming here for the summer. Convenient for Dad, too, of course.'

She stopped, surprised at herself. Annoyed, even. They stood there in silence for a few moments. Normally Cassie was fine with silences, but this time she felt the need to fill it.

'Alex said you're a travel photographer or something now?'

She heard her voice stressing the word 'now' – as in, 'my, what a long way you've come from here.' Sometimes she could hear how she must sound to other people – brisk, sharp, condescending – but she couldn't do anything about it even if she'd wanted to. He gave a quick, amused smile, totally at ease. *I don't have the power to affect him.* It bothered her.

'Yeah – or something. Alex might have exaggerated a bit. I just like to keep moving. If I stay still, then...'

He shrugged. His face looked faraway for a moment. Had he been happy growing up in this place, ever, or had he always wanted to get away and be something else? *Everyone has something they want, or need.*

From the kitchen came the sound of ice clinking against glass.

'So, do you still live around here – when you're not off taking photos, I mean?'

'Actually, I haven't been back here for years; just like you two, so I hear. My parents are dead now, so not much point really.'

'I heard. Sorry.'

'Thanks – it was a while ago now. Dad went and then Mum kind of gave up. Happens a lot, so I'm told.'

The door to the sitting room opened and Alex was standing there, holding a jug of something violently pink.

'There you are, Cass. I made daiquiris,' she said. 'Sit and have a drink with us, why don't you? Be sociable for once, like you used to be. Could you grab some glasses from the dresser?'

Cassie moved away from Joe and picked up three glasses. Drink, yes, that was probably what she needed more than anything. Only, when she took the first gulp from hers, she almost choked.

'Jesus, Alex. What have you put in it?'

'This and that.' She raised her glass, meeting Joe's eyes. 'Cheers.'

Joe lifted his glass. 'See you on the other side, I guess.'

Cassie sank down on the deep, burgundy sofa that sagged in the middle and took another generous swallow of the cloying pink concoction. This time she was prepared for it, and the warmth spread all the way down to her tingling feet.

'So what kind of pictures do you take, Joe?'

'Joe takes pictures for *National Geographic*,' said Alex. 'They pay him a fortune.'

He laughed. 'I wouldn't say that. I'm a freelancer actually; I work for lots of people. What about you, Cassie? Alex tells me you're a writer, or something, now.' His eyes were faintly mocking, she thought, as he echoed her words from earlier.

'Of sorts. I write about other people's books. I guess you could say I'm a freelancer too.'

'A critic then?'

'Yes.'

'Cassie's been trying to write a novel for years,' interjected Alex, 'but she's never quite finished it, have you, Cass? She's clever, you see, Joe. Much more than me; I've never been academic.'

Fishing, fishing... be careful, Alex – you never know what you might catch around here.

'Oh, Cassie, remember how I told you I found this in the cupboard?'

Cassie watched as Alex triumphantly produced Lucie's record player.

'Does it even work?'

'It did the other day. Lucie would want us to use it. Remember how she loved her music.'

Cassie sank further back on the sofa and stretched her body, reaching her bare arms up over her head, feeling her muscles tighten as she clenched her fists. She watched with a sense of inevitability as Alex set the player up on the table and selected a Sinatra record – it was the old songs Lucie had adored – then her sister jumped up and was dancing, alone, completely caught up for a moment in her own body, and Cassie envied her that. She envied the knowing delight Alex took in her own form. She poured more drink. And then, as Cassie had known she would, Alex reached out her arms to Joe.

'Come *on*. Come and dance with me.'

'*... But why should I try to resist, when baby I know so well...*'

He protested for a moment, then allowed himself to be pulled up, and they spun around together. Cassie watched them and drank, feeling slightly voyeuristic. She'd been in this situation before, and she knew Alex probably *wanted* it to be a performance. *Look, I caught another one. He's mine now, not yours.* Sometimes, sometimes, she thought that Alex's whole life was a performance and that there was another Alex that she'd never met, waiting offstage. Waiting for someone to notice, or rescue, her.

Feverishly, Alex changed the music – could never stick with one thing for long. Bobby Darin now, wasn't it? She pulled Joe to her again, and as Cassie watched, the two of them were becoming blurred, like they were combining into one. She rolled back her head and blinked her eyes back into focus as the music pulled her irresistibly into the past and just like earlier she had to struggle to get her head above the waterline before she drowned in it. She blinked and tried to sit upright.

'*Somewhere, beyond the sea...*'

And then the lights went off and the music cut out and some kind of spell had been broken.

'What happened?' Alex's voice was thick, a little slurred. 'Did you do that, Cass, you witch? Or was it Bella? It was Bella, wasn't it? BELLA,' she shouted up at the ceiling. Then she bent forward and whispered in Joe's ear. 'She hated us, you know. She doesn't want us here. She killed the woman down the road's dog, you know.' And then she started giggling, manically.

'It'll be the fuse,' said Joe. 'If you show me where the box is, I can look at it.'

'No need,' said Cassie, testing her feet and pulling herself up. Not so drunk, after all. 'I know where it is; I know what to do.'

She made her way carefully along the hallway to the fuse box under the stairs, shining her phone to guide her and stop her from falling over her stupid feet. As she'd known, the switches had flipped down; something had tripped. Old house. Messed-up wiring. Faulty connections. She pushed them up again and the lights turned on.

But it had altered the mood back in the room. Alex and Joe were now standing at the front window overlooking the driveway.

'What is it?'

'I think there was someone out there.'

Alex's eyes were very bright, her pupils dilated.

'Don't suppose they had a pram, did they?' Cassie said it absently – half to herself – and then instantly regretted it.

'What *are* you talking about?' said Alex.

'Nothing – nothing.'

Alex's eyes narrowed, suddenly alert again. 'You're being cagey, Cass.'

'I'm not being cagey.'

'Tell me or I'll – I'll *set Bella on you*.' She began giggling again. She wasn't the kind to let up.

'For God's sake, Alex. Alright, do you remember a woman standing outside the shop the other day with a baby?'

'No. Why?'

'I recognised her then and then I saw her – I thought I saw her again today on the road, that's all, OK? Remember the little girl we used to play with sometimes when we were kids? The daughter of that woman who cleaned the house.'

Alex screwed up her face for a moment and put her head on one side.

'You mean the one who...'

'Yes.'

Alex turned to Joe.

'She was always following us around – cute little thing though. What was her name, Cass – Bobby, Belinda?'

'Billie.'

'That's right. But you're wrong, it can't have been her. Because I remember Lucie saying about it – she was never right after that accident. I heard they moved away or they took her away somewhere or something and then that was it.'

'I'm sure you're right. I imagine I got it wrong. Like I said, it doesn't matter anyway.'

'What happened to her?' said Joe.

'An accident – at least, would you call it that, Cass?'

'Shut up, Alex.'

'I'm surprised you don't know, Joe. I thought everyone knew about everything around here. It's like this: We were on the beach one day. When we were kids, this little girl used to hang around with us sometimes while her mum was cleaning the house. Bloody Bella wouldn't leave us alone that day, but wasn't it – didn't you shout at her to go away, Cassie? Because of something that had happened? In the attic.'

Cassie continued to look out the window. There was a light flickering across the fields in the distance. She clenched her fists.

'I don't remember.' But again, in her head, she heard Alex's laughter from behind the locked attic door all those years ago, and now she thought: *One day she's going to cause real damage.*

'You must do; come on, Cass. Anyway, like I said, we were on the beach and we were trying to build some kind of massive trench in the sand – stupid really, but then there wasn't that much to do those days – and Bella came along and stood in it and you said – you said, "Go away, Bella, this is ours," you said. And then she looked at Cassie for a moment, a bit like the way Cassie's looking at me now, because I can see your face in the window, Cass – and then she grabbed a manky old doll that Billie was holding and just ran off towards the cliff, and the kid watched her for a second and then went hurtling off after her crying and screaming before we could stop her. Remember, Cass? That doll she used to carry around with her everywhere. Tatty thing it was, but then I think she was a bit odd – bit simple, or something. Anyway, Bella starts to climb the cliffs. Remember, Cass, how she could climb like something that wasn't human? But then she wasn't human, that cousin of ours. She was so strong and there were all these tufts of grass or something sticking out of the cliff and she was grabbing on to them to climb up and you were – you were shouting at her to come down, that she'd fall onto the rocks below, but all the time...'

All the time a part of me was hoping she'd fall so somehow we'd all be free. Free from what, though? From who?

'… all the time she just kept going. She got to that part where a bit of flat rock is sticking out and she sat there, holding the doll out and then the – Billie was below there and she started shouting to her, and Bella said, "Climb up, follow me up here, unless you're scared." Bella didn't talk all that much and I'm glad, because she had that horrible voice, didn't she? It was all… dead, or flat, or something. And anyway, it was like Billie – like she got possessed with this rage, you know how little kids get, and so she started climbing up after her, and it all happened so fast and we should have stopped her but we didn't get there in time and she had these spindly little arms and they looked like they were going to break. You said you were going to run and get Lucie or her mum to stop her. And the whole bloody time Bella was smiling this horrible smile, like when she got up there she was going to eat her. Eat her alive, and then… but Jesus, that wasn't the only thing Bella did. She wasn't allowed to even *be* around little kids on her own, was she? Not after that time Lucie's friends came over from France with their baby and…'

She paused to take a breath. Her voice was trembling now, like she was going to cry, and Cassie wished the music was playing again.

And right then, there was a noise from upstairs, like something moving around. Footsteps. Cassie imagined them coming slowly down the stairs; she imagined it was Bella, not dead after all. She'd just been waiting like a spider all those years for the right time to crawl from the shadows and get her revenge on them all for… Bella, moving slowly, inch by inch, reaching out to grab the door handle, silently hating them.

She could feel her breath coming out, harder and harder, and her fists were clenched so tight now her arms were shaking; she knew she was going to shout at Alex soon. She was going to scream in her face to go away to rejoin the party and leave her here on her own with… She turned to face her sister to say what she really wanted to say to her…

'What happened?'

She snapped her head around; she'd forgotten Joe was in the room. He'd become as irrelevant right then as the pebbles outside on the driveway or those faraway lights across the fields. For a moment it had just been her and Alex and their family skeletons dancing in the lamplight. He was looking between them both, curious, slightly apprehensive, like he was waiting for one of them to shatter into pieces all over the floor but he couldn't decide which it was going to be.

'What happened when?'

They'd both almost forgotten.

'I mean, what happened with the little girl?'

Cassie met Alex's too-bright eyes and held her gaze for a moment, aware of the challenge in there. Then she took a breath and finished the story for her in as deliberately straightforward a way as she could.

'She fell, of course. She fell and she smashed her face up on the rocks, and it damaged her brain in some way, they said. They said she needed steel pins just to put her back together again, like a doll. Oh, and the doll? Bella threw it down and its face got cracked too, as it goes. She threw it right before Billie reached her.'

Her face smashed like a shell, and all because she tried to follow Bella, and maybe Bella took her doll because I'd told her to go away and made her angry with us all. She swallowed the spider to catch the fly.

Alex seemed to have recovered herself and was fiddling around with the music again, almost as though nothing had happened. She was quick to forget, when she was in this state. Quick, as ever, to dip in and out of moods.

Finally, she looked up, eyes gleaming.

'I know, Joe – let's go for a late-night swim. Come on.' She grabbed him by the arm and he gave an easy laugh, shaking his head.

'Why not? I need to go to the bathroom first, though. Is it upstairs?'

'That's it. Round to the right.'

He left the room, and Cassie and Alex were alone.

'He's compliant.'

'Shut up, Cass, you're just jealous.'

'I'm honestly not.'

They stood in semi-hostile silence. The time seemed to go on and on, and Cassie was about to ask whether he'd got lost, but then they heard footsteps coming down the stairs.

'Ready,' he said. 'Are you coming too, Cassie?'

'I don't think so; I'm tired.'

'Come on then, Joe, let's go now,' said Alex. 'Don't wait up for us, Cass.'

Alex pulled him out of the room, and he barely had time to say goodbye. Soon Cassie heard the door slam.

'Don't drown,' she said softly.

And now she was left alone in the house, but that was OK because the noises were only noises. Taking a deep breath, she picked up the remains of her drink and took it up the stairs with her, holding on to the banister; unsure, now, of her step. *Used to be so graceful. Used to feel my feet.*

Once she got to the top, rather than turning left into her room, she stopped and looked around her, scanning the dark corners.

There and then she made a decision: tomorrow she was going to start clearing out this house which was, after all, why she was supposed to be here. And she'd start by bringing down Bella's revolting box of dead crab claws and throwing them back into the sea where they belonged.

That would show her.

This time, the noise came from her aunt's room, on the other side of the stairwell. She only hesitated a moment before going towards it. She'd avoided going in there since that first day, but the door was open, and she got the feeling that someone had been in here recently because the bedsheets looked ruffled. Alex, probably. She didn't even need to turn the light on because the moon tonight was bright enough to see by. The lack of curtains made it colder at night, somehow sadder, and the windows were like unseeing eyes. This house was uneven, juddery. Was it swaying backwards and forwards when they were in it, without them realising it? When she had that feeling of vertigo, was that where it was coming from? The house itself?

'You're waiting to pitch us over the cliff, aren't you?' she said out loud to the walls, the violent pink booze making her entirely unselfconscious.

Lucie had hated this house. Hated it. And yet she had stayed. Cassie kept coming back to this fact, and she could never find a satisfactory reason why. She was going to have to ask Mrs Gibbett the questions she'd been avoiding. She was going to have to ask her about the day Lucie died, because it felt wrong – not knowing.

Then she turned back to the naked window, and her throat constricted.

There was a figure out on the gravelled drive, standing motionless, face turned up to her. Alex was right. There *had* been someone there.

She realised who it was: Mrs Gibbett. Fucking Mrs Gibbett, out by herself in the middle of the night for some reason of her own.

Better not go down to the beach, Mrs G. Might see more than you bargained for. Cassie waited for her to move on, but the woman continued to stand there, looking up at the bedroom. *Does she see me?*

Cassie thought about putting up her hand to wave, but something stopped her. Slowly, the woman began to shake her head, very deliberately, from side to side as though in sorrow or disappointment. The moment seemed to last three lifetimes, but it couldn't have been more than a few seconds. Then she turned and walked back down the path to her house, and Cassie watched her until she had disappeared into the shadows.

There was something not right about that woman.

She turned to look around the room, and again the sense of Lucie's absence hit her like a crushing wave.

'It's your fault, Bella,' she said out loud. 'It's your fault she pushed us away. Tomorrow I'm going to throw your box into the sea, do you hear me?'

She sank down on Lucie's bed and held on to one of the pillows and then suddenly there was that damn scratching again and it got louder and louder, so she put the pillow over her head to muffle it until, eventually, she fell asleep.

10

'Come and see this, Cass.'

Cassie, sitting at the kitchen table with a mug in front of her, looked up from the book she was supposed to be reading; some kind of ghost story.

'Cass, did you hear me? Put that book down and come and look.'

It was the next afternoon and Alex, as was typical for her, seemed to have forgotten about the previous night.

Cassie had no idea how long Joe had stayed or if he'd left at all; she'd slept there on Lucie's bed until morning and she'd woken up stiff, one arm numb, the dawn seeping through the windows. And then, before she'd even had time to think about it, she'd gone straight upstairs to the attic and emptied out that box of dismembered claws into a plastic bag and strode out into the grey morning light to empty them back into the sea. She'd watched some sink, some disintegrate and some bob away on the waves, wrapping her bare arms around herself and feeling the cold saltwater lap over her feet. Right there and then, she'd been the only person in the world.

There you are, Bella, she'd thought. *What do you say to that?*

But when she'd turned around to go back, it was already getting lighter and she saw she wasn't the only person out there after all. There was somebody on the cliff, right at the end of the garden, looking directly at her. Her breath caught in her throat; she watched as it extended one hand towards her. Was she *always* being watched now? For a moment she started to panic because she thought, *They'll fall* – and then for a second it was her falling...

She'd shaken her head angrily and looked away. When she looked back it was as she'd known it would be; the figure had gone. It was just her mind playing tricks on her again; the early morning light; fears conjuring up hallucinations – whatever you wanted to blame it on.

All in your head, see? Just like they told you.

She pushed herself up from the table, waiting for the rush of blood to subside. She was not hungover, exactly, but there was a certain residual lightheadedness, like someone had been extracting bits of her brain during the night.

She joined her sister at the window. Alex smelled like expensive perfume. *I sleep in Chanel No. 5*, she heard Marilyn say in a fluttering voice. Alex would love to be Marilyn, only she was too much of a waif.

'What am I looking at?' Cassie asked.

'Over there, on the sand.'

It was just possible to see the beach from here, beyond the sand dunes. Cassie directed her eyes to where Alex was pointing, squinting them into focus, and saw a dark, bulky shape, just where the sea met the shore.

'What is it?'

'I don't know. It's big, isn't it?'

'It wasn't there earlier when I went out for a walk. We should go and look.'

'Should we? What if it's something horrible?'

'What if it is?'

Alex would come anyway because she wouldn't be able to help herself. She was one of the most curious people Cassie had ever known, like a little bird that couldn't stop pecking at a worm until it'd been pulled to pieces.

The two of them made their way down the path towards the shape, whatever it was. (Cassie's mind went back to the figure on the cliff that morning. But no, that hadn't been real.) They were both barefoot, and the sand was warm and gritty. There was nobody else around so they'd be the first ones to discover whatever it was. Maybe this was how it had felt to discover the first dinosaur bones.

When they got nearer, there was a smell, like rotten seaweed, even though Cassie couldn't be sure she'd ever encountered rotten seaweed before and didn't even actually know if it *did* rot. She took a deep breath, and as she did so, she felt Alex clutch her arm.

'Ow.'

'Oh Jesus, what is it?' said Alex, wrinkling up her nose.

Cassie stepped away from Alex and got a little closer, putting her hand over her mouth. The thing had barnacles on it. Something had already been eating it. Her stomach turned over.

'It looks like a whale. Poor thing.'

Alex went closer now, and Cassie almost thought she gave a sigh of relief. Something splashed over her bare foot. The sea was rolling, and she looked up to see dark clouds gathering. Was there a storm coming – finally, after all these days and weeks of endless sun?

'You'll tell me I'm stupid, Cass, but, for a moment there at the window, I thought it was a body – a person, you know – and do you know what I thought? It'll sound insane, but I thought, oh, Bella's finally washed up after all these years and it'll be my fault if she comes to get me for all the bad things I said about her.'

Cassie gave a chuckle, but only because for one illogical moment – but what was one more of those among many, these past few weeks? – she'd thought it, too. Only she didn't, of course, acknowledge this to Alex. Instead, she said, nodding at the sky:

'I think it's going to rain.'

'Finally,' said Alex.

It was then that Cassie felt something run over her feet, something that wasn't the cold water of the North Sea. Something sharp, that scuttled. She looked down to see a huge, orange-red crab.

'Cassie, what's...?'

And then Cassie saw them coming out of the sea – big ones, small ones, all different colours, like an army. Another one came up from under the sand, right near her twitching big toe. The rational part of her knew this wasn't happening, but they kept coming, and coming, and she couldn't move because her legs had turned to lead again, and she thought, *I'm going to drown in them like quicksand and then later on the ground will spew out the tattered bits of what's left of me.* She looked up at the sky and the clouds were gathering, and then, all at once, they burst in a biblical downpour. Alex, with a squeal, had started to retreat along the sand, half laughing.

'Cassie, come *on*, we're going to get drenched.'

She allowed herself to be pulled away, and the two of them ran back up the beach to the cliff path. She hadn't run for a long time, and it was exhilarating to find she still, in fact, could. Despite everything, she felt a sudden giddy elation, and as she looked at Alex, she knew she felt it too. The two of them fell down on the sand just before they reached the path up the dunes and began to laugh, with a tinge of hysteria, and they laughed until they couldn't breathe because, in that moment, it was the only thing to do.

'The size of that thing...' gasped Alex, her pixie hair all plastered down by the rain.

Eventually, they got up, still laughing – the first real laugh they'd shared together for years – and climbed up the cliff path to the house. Cassie felt lighter, freer. *Maybe things really are possible for me – for us – after all.*

But when they got to the house, the laughter caught in Cassie's throat. Lucie was lying on the doorstep, but she didn't look up in greeting, her yellow eyes blinking in expectation of her next meal, her next stroke; she lay stiff, motionless.

It was the second dead thing they'd encountered that day.

II

Alex got to her first. She knelt down in front of the pile of rain-soaked orange fur and gathered her up.

'Lucie,' she said, 'Lucie,' shaking her, like it was going to wake her up.

The cat's mouth was still slightly open, little sharp teeth and pink gums exposed.

I didn't like cats anyway, thought Cassie. *I didn't like them anyway.* She clenched her jaw.

Alex was now crying dainty little sobs that shuddered down to her sun-browned feet, holding Lucie over her shoulder like she was a newborn baby. The ants had already found her; Cassie could see them dispersing from the spot where she'd been lying, and some of them were crawling from her paws and onto Alex's top. As Alex sat on the ground in the rain, Cassie looked at the scene, a feeling of terrible guilt bearing down on her, as though somehow she had caused this to happen. A little way down the road, she saw a figure pushing a pram before it disappeared out of sight around the bend.

'Oh, my dears; oh, the poor thing. What happened?'

It was Mrs Gibbett, of course. Her big, doughy face was looking down at them in concern, feet planted wide and encased in those huge wellingtons. How was it that she always turned up when you least wanted her – like she was watching, watching all the time? Cassie's mind wandered back to the previous night, to the shock of feeling she was being observed through Lucie's window, and by whom.

Alex, still holding the dead cat, looked up at Mrs Gibbet with wild eyes and said, 'Someone did something to her.'

The woman stared at her. 'No. Surely not?'

'Alex,' said Cassie slowly, carefully, like you would talk to a child. 'I think she was an old cat.'

The woman looked down at the cat on the ground again, shaking her head. 'Well, I don't know – I find it hard to believe…' Then she straightened up. 'In any case, you can't sit out here in the rain. Tell you what, take yourselves inside and I'll put this poor thing in the shed for now. Then I'll make you a cup of tea, that's what I'll do.'

'Be gentle with her,' said Alex.

The woman picked up the pile of beautiful, orange fur and disappeared around the back of the house. Alex, shoulders hunched over and with a mixture of tears and rain running down her face, opened the kitchen door and Cassie followed her in. Almost in tandem, the two of them sat heavily at the table. Alex stared down at the uneven wooden boards. Cassie examined a spider on the floor, thinking, *Lucie might have caught that and eaten it if she'd been in here.* Lucie had never brought in any mice or birds, but she'd seemed to have a particular vendetta against arachnids.

Uninvited but sure of her welcome in a time of grieving, Mrs Gibbett bustled after them into the kitchen, shut the door and picked up the kettle.

'You need sweet tea,' she said. 'It's good when you've had a bit of a shock, so they say.'

Alex was crying again; her tears were dripping onto the table and staining the wood darker brown.

'What did you do with her?' said Cassie.

'I put her safely in a box with the lid on, until you decide what you want to do with her body. There's a pet crematorium a way down the road, you know.'

'We're going to bury her properly,' said Alex. 'She's not going to be sent away to be burned like rubbish just because she was only a stray cat.'

Why not? They burned the other Lucie.

The woman had her back to them. She was opening the cupboard above the kettle to find mugs, and then there was a smash.

'Oh, crumbs,' she said. 'I'm so sorry, girls, I'm glad that wasn't one of your aunt's special ones. The handle just came away.'

It was then Cassie noticed that the woman's hands were shaking. *Of course*, she thought, *she's probably remembering the dog*. For a moment she felt that aggravating, niggling burst of almost-pity; they'd become attached to Lucie the cat in a way, but that dog had probably been the woman's only live-in companion her whole life. Was there ever even a Mr Gibbett? Funny, she'd never even thought about it. She glanced at Alex, and she knew, for once, that they were thinking the same thing. Alex had stopped crying, and she was chewing her bottom lip.

But Mrs Gibbett knows things about Lucie, or she knows more than we do anyway – you're sure of it now, aren't you?

'Never mind about the tea,' said Cassie suddenly. 'I think we need something a bit stronger.'

'Well, I don't know. I don't usually drink, and certainly not this early in the day, but...'

'Why don't you sit at the table with Alex and I'll make us all a drink.'

Cassie went into the living room to pick up the gin (*Auntie's Ruin*) and some glasses. Back in the kitchen, she mixed up strong gin and tonics for each of them. Outside, the rain was still pouring down; the window over the sink clearly wasn't sealed properly anymore because some of the water was seeping through.

'Well – thank you,' said Mrs Gibbett, raising her glass with a steadier hand. 'Here's to absent friends.'

After a pause while they all held their glasses aloft, Cassie said slowly, carefully, 'I hope this doesn't bring back bad memories for you. About your little dog, I mean. I remember it happening all those years ago. That awful thing our cousin did.'

Cassie watched as though from a distance as the woman's body stiffened; she watched her lean back and her eyes almost go in on themselves, like she was going back to another time. She took a deep drink from her glass, pulling a face.

'Goodness, that's strong. Yes – yes, of course; you're very kind to remember about him. Poor little Rexie.'

'It would be hard to forget; I was there that day, remember?'

Alex stared with her mouth open, tears apparently forgotten. What are you *doing*? said her eyes.

The woman's face had hardened now, in a way Cassie had never quite seen it do before. It was stiff, waxen, her thin lips compressed. Perhaps this was her real face, the one she wore when she was on her own and there was no need to be neighbourly. *Because we all wear a different face when we're on our own, you know that better than anyone.*

The woman wiped her eyes and took another slug of her drink, but when she spoke, all she said was, 'It's nice, this; all girls together.'

Cassie topped up their glasses without asking. She felt Alex kick her under the table, and she thought, *There'll be a bruise there tomorrow, and it will spread and spread and then it will go black.* She looked up at her sister and shook her head. Alex shrugged and turned to look out of the window; it was still raining.

'Did you never want to know why?' said Cassie softly.

The woman looked straight at her now. 'Sometimes there isn't any why, my dear.' She shook her head, and she also looked out of the window.

Word must have already got round somehow about the washed-up whale on the beach; every now and then people came past the window on their way to the dune path, far more than on a usual day. Probably the most interesting thing that had ever washed up here.

Alex picked up the bottle and poured herself another drink, then she stood up, like she was about to leave the room – like she was bored or depressed by this conversation – but suddenly Mrs Gibbett turned to them and spoke again.

'Your aunt did the best she could with that girl, you know. Oh, she was a remarkable woman – I didn't blame her for what happened. No, not at all.'

Cassie spoke quietly. 'Remarkable – yes. But Lucie was so private about so many things. We still don't know anything at all about her last years, after Bella was gone. Why she end-ed up back here in this big house all on her own. Because the Lucie we knew *loved* having people around her. I remember those friends of hers who used to come to stay for days on end, and they all seemed so... so sophisticated to me.'

'Hmm,' said the woman, her mouth pursed, eyes fixed a little unnervingly now on Cassie's face.

'You must have missed her, in a way, when she left for a while. After Bella died, I mean,' said Cassie.

'Well, yes, but then of course, she didn't stay away long. I knew she wouldn't be able to. I knew she'd come back to stay and she did and she stayed right up until – well, you know.'

'I'm surprised she came back at all. I'm surprised she didn't leave for good.'

'Oh, she did talk about going away again but at the end of the day, it was just talk. All this business about how *this* time she was going to leave and never come back, and it was a place that brought nothing but... it got to how most days she said it but somehow, she never quite did, almost like she was waiting for something. And I have to say that, selfishly, I'd have... been sad to see her go away again.'

'*Was* she waiting for something?'

The spider was crawling up the wall near the door now; it had reached the height of the woman's head. It had a thick, black body, and from here Cassie could almost see the hairs on its legs. She wondered if it was pregnant.

'You'll have to forgive me, but your aunt didn't share much with people, although it's true, dare I say it' – here, the woman gave a sort of horribly girlish titter, nothing like the deep boom she usually made that passed for a laugh – 'she let me in a little more than most, you might say.'

Her eyes drifted off again, remembering, perhaps, those gifted years.

Cassie took a breath. 'It must have been a shock for you – when it happened. It was a shock for us to hear about it. When Lucie died, I mean. The accident. We should have talked to you about it before – asked about it. You must find it strange that we didn't.'

'Oh, but why would you want to dwell on that? I'm old, I've seen some things in my time, but you girls... Well, it was a horrible... accident. Horrible.' She shuddered.

'I'd like to know about it now, if you don't mind.'

'Are you really sure?'

'I'd like to.'

Mrs Gibbett closed her eyes tight for a moment and then opened them again and shook her head. She put her hands down flat on the table and took a deep breath like she'd been remembering her lines. Finally, she said:

'Well... that day I was walking up the path to the house, just coming to see if your aunt needed anything doing because, well, I'd got into the habit of doing that in those last months. I rather think she needed me, in fact. Only, when I went in there, she wasn't in the house, and I knew then that she must be down by the cliff at the end of the garden.'

'Why there?'

'She'd become sort of... bothered by the way the cliff was falling away there. She kept on and on going to check it, and I'd say to her, "There's nothing you can do about it, there's nothing any of us can do about it. It's just nature," but she still kept going, although I thought in her condition she had to be careful.'

'Condition? What condition?' Cassie kept her voice low and steady.

'Well, that's it, I don't rightly know. She was a private person, as I'm sure you recall, but I knew something wasn't right. That she wasn't well at all. It wasn't my place to say anything, and, her being her, she didn't want people to know.'

'I don't quite understand.'

'It came on gradually, you see, in bits and pieces. She just seemed to be... Fading is the only way I can describe it. It got so she couldn't even walk along the beach every day the way she loved to – remember?'

Cassie remembered. Looking out of the window and watching Lucie walking barefoot on the sand in the morning with her dress swishing, and all was safe and right, even if there was Bella somewhere up in the attic like a goblin.

'The sand was too much for her. I think she thought I didn't notice. Oh, maybe I should have said something. Should have spoken up.'

She looked at Cassie expectantly, as though waiting for her to deny it.

'Didn't she go to the doctor or anything?'

'I think she may well have done, but – well, you know what doctors can be like. Not worth the money they spend on all those years of training, some of them.'

'No.'

(*Sitting in the doctor's office, over and over again, all those months.*

'*Can you tell me what you're experiencing?*'

'*It started with tingling, but constantly. Then there was this numbness that seemed to spread.*'

The doctor has a serious-but-reassuring expression on his face. Oh, he's seen it all before. Overwrought, probably, he's thinking. He's seen her notes.

'*I see.*'

'*And then there are the... flashes. Like there's something in the corner of my eye but when I turn around it's gone. And I get these headaches. Sometimes it's like someone is putting a tight band around my head and pulling and pulling. And I'm having really vivid nightmares, but not now and then. All the time.*'

'*And how long has this been going on for?*'

He asks several more questions like this, checks her reflexes and makes her get up and perform some kind of dressage. Walking along one foot in front of the other, ankle to toe, like a tightrope walker.

Finally, he concludes, 'Cassandra, I think you've been under a lot of stress.'

'*I don't feel stressed.*'

'*Sometimes things manifest themselves in other ways.*'

'*You're telling me none of this is real?*'

'*I can't find anything physically wrong with you. Nobody has.*')

And the woman was going on, her voice the tiniest bit slurred:

'But then, you see, that's when we became – closer, I suppose you might even call it. She came to rely on me, as I say. Those friends of hers you talked about – well, they'd long since stopped coming. Perhaps she didn't want them to see her or maybe they weren't interested if there was no fun to be had. Or maybe she didn't want them in this house after everything that happened because, well, sometimes places get a... stain on them, do you see? I sometimes thought – it will seem stupid, I know – oh, listen to me going on – not used to drinking. My mother always said, "You talk too much, girl. Keep your tongue in your head," she'd say.'

'Why didn't you tell someone if you knew she was ill? *Why didn't you try to contact one of us?*'

'But she would have been *furious*,' she said, like it was obvious. 'Can you imagine?' The woman shook her head as though picturing the fury that would have rained down on her. 'Perhaps if she'd gone on and got worse and worse I might have done, but then there was the... the accident. So, as I said, that day I went out into the garden to see if she was there at the edge of the cliff, only, just as I got round the corner, I heard the most awful sound – it was, like a scream but angrier; more like a howl? Oh, but what does it matter how it sounded – so of course I rushed up and she turned... she turned to look at me or maybe up at the house, I don't know, and then she... oh mercy, she slipped.' She passed a hand over her forehead. 'I rushed to look over at her to see if she'd... and you don't... well, you don't want to know what I saw. So I ran to call an ambulance and then I ran down to the beach, but... you know it's *what* she screamed – I could have sworn she said – and it made me think...' She shook her head, like she was trying to shake the memories off.

'And we never knew.'

'Well, my dears, like you said – I said – she was so proud and she'd have hated for just anyone to know when she was weak.'

Just anyone? Cassie couldn't say anything right away, couldn't get the words out. A white flame of rage rose up inside her. But when she finally spoke, her voice remained steady, years of control doing their work.

'But we're not just anyone; *we're* her family.'

She put an emphasis on the 'we're', drawing an exclusionary ring round herself and Alex. She felt an irresistible urge to be cruel, to hit out and hurt; never mind about the dog now. What *right* had this woman to take care of Lucie, after all?

'It's funny,' she went on. 'Lucie always said things to me like, "Poor Mrs Gibbett – but sometimes we have to tolerate people, if only to be kind." I suppose Lucie *was* kind. But then you were the only one around in the end; it's strange how life goes.'

The half-smile stayed on Mrs Gibbett's face, exactly as it had been before, as she stared at Cassie and the words hung in the air between them. And then:

'Ah, well,' she said softly. 'Ah, well. None of it matters now really, of course.'

Slowly, she heaved herself to her feet.

'I'm sorry, my dears, I really don't know what came over me; I'm not used to drinking, and that poor old moggie... Well, very upsetting for you both. I ought to go now; so much to do for the carnival tomorrow. There's always so much to do.'

She leaned on the doorframe for a few moments to steady herself, before pulling on her muddy wellingtons she'd stood so carefully by the door on her way in.

'But you didn't finish what you were saying,' said Cassie.

'When?'

'You were telling us that Lucie shouted something, right before she had the accident – before she fell. What was it?'

'Oh, I really don't know...'

'Please.'

'Bella,' said the woman. 'I think it was Bella.' She shook her head. 'All those years, and perhaps she never really got over it.'

Then Mrs Gibbett left, and they watched her trudge, slowly, carefully, past the window, through the puddles that had collected. Over on the beach, Cassie could see a collection of people huddled around the dead whale. The spider had reached the ceiling. The rainwater was still seeping in through the rotten kitchen window frames and had formed a little river going towards the sink.

Alex pushed her chair back and stood. Cassie looked up at her, expecting to see tears in her eyes, but instead, her sister's face was a shocking, glass-eyed blank.

'I hope you've heard enough now. I hope that satisfies your curiosity.'

'Wouldn't you rather know?'

'What do we know that I – we didn't know already? Lucie's dead. They're both dead and we're alive, and yet somehow you refuse to have any kind of life. Sometimes I feel like I'm doing all the living for both of us while you're... Oh, fuck it – what's the point?'

Alex left the room and Cassie heard light footsteps running up the stairs. The room went in and out of focus. She realised that, yet again, she couldn't feel her feet and the wound on her hand was throbbing and itching and burning. She'd taken to rubbing at the skin around the bandage, and it was starting to look red and sore. She'd have to take the dressing off and look at it at some point, only she didn't want to because in some way she was afraid of what she would see.

What's wrong? Afraid that all the rot and bitterness inside you is working its way to the surface finally? Zombie-woman.

She poured herself another large drink and reached into her pocket for one of her pills.

Mrs Gibbett said Lucie had been ill. Even before the accident, she was ill. Was she afraid? Did she know what it was? Could Cassie have done anything?

Am I to blame for this, too?

The hand that was holding the drink was shaking. Upstairs, a door slammed heavily and then there was a thud from the hallway, and she looked over to see that a part of one of the mouldings on the ceiling had come loose and fallen to the floor.

Bella. She shouted Bella. That's what the woman said.

And in the very corner – that fleeting periphery – of her mind's eye she saw that figure standing on the cliff.

12

They buried Lucie in the evening, while it was still light but the midges were dancing around them; *that* kind of light. They made a hole at the end of the garden, behind the fence before the jagged edge of the cliff. One day her little body would fall down onto the beach below but it wouldn't matter by then. They didn't speak very much afterwards, as they stood there looking down at the mound of earth. Hard to know exactly what they were grieving for, thought Cassie.

'Bye, Lucie,' said Alex. And then she turned abruptly and went back into the darkening house.

13

'Wake up, Cass! The sun's shining again and the rain's cleaned all the shittiness away.'

Cassie opened her eyes and blinked up at her sister shimmering in a designer sundress and those jewelled sandals with a high, excited look on her face. She jumped on the end of Cassie's bed and bounced like it was Christmas. No point in Cassie telling her she'd been awake most of the night.

'What is it?' she said.

'It's the carnival in town today. You can't have forgotten – every bloody soul in this place has been banging on about it since we got here.'

She stared at her sister. Had yesterday been a dream?

'Alex, I didn't want to go to the damn carnival at the best of times, but after yesterday...'

'No. We're going to go. We're going to get dressed up and we're going to look gorgeous and we're going to find a pub to watch it all from and get properly pissed – shots and everything – and toast Lucie. Joe said he'd meet me – us.' Her eyes had that determined gleam Cassie knew well.

'Is that what we're going to do?'

'Come on, Cass. You haven't even tried to look nice since you got here. The next bus is in an hour and we're getting on it.'

Alex fluttered out of the room and Cassie heard her cantering down the stairs. She lay there for a moment, flexing her fingers and toes and feeling like the world had tilted somehow since yesterday.

I'm not going. Alex can piss off.

But then her eyes travelled down her body, rigid after a tense, sleepless night. She looked down at her long legs and her flat stomach and she felt a shift. All at once, she *admired* herself as she hadn't done for what must have been years. Alex was right, in a way – it had been a long time since she'd felt beautiful, but possibly she *was* beautiful. People had often told her so, and they couldn't all be wrong. She stretched her legs out and ran her hands down her body and then dug her nails into her thighs.

Fuck it all. Fuck everyone and everything. The sun was shining like it did every day and Lucie was gone like she was every day, just like Mother, just like lots of people. So she pulled herself out of bed, naked and pale, and then, very deliberately, she padded across the landing to Lucie's room, where she opened up the huge, ornate wardrobe with roses carved on the front and looked through it until she found a green silk dress with a low back. Then she did her eyes in shimmering gold and put on some red lipstick – Lucie's favourite colour – that she found in the dressing-table drawer. She stopped to examine her pale skin in the mirror, angling her face to catch the light on her cheekbones. All these people had told her she looked like Lucie, but even now she couldn't see it. All she saw was Cassie putting on Lucie, dressing in Lucie. All the same, she leaned over and touched hands with this Lucie-her and placed a kiss on the mirror, on the red mouth reflected there. When she stood back, it had left an imprint on the glass, and she stared at it for a while until she was pulled out of herself by the sound of Alex calling her name.

***

Downstairs, in the kitchen, Alex looked her up and down, half admiring, half disapproving.

'I said look nice; I didn't say look *too* nice. I didn't say look sexy.'

Cassie smiled at her, suddenly blissfully uncaring. Today she was going away from this house. Today, just for today, she was going to be free of everything. Already, she felt lighter at the thought of it.

'You said to make an effort.'

'Here,' said Alex, holding out a pill.

'What is it?'

'Just something to loosen you up. We're going to have fun today, Cass, me and you. We're going to forget about all the horribleness, and then...'

'Then what?'

'Then maybe it's time to leave here and go back to our lives?'

'You first.'

'No. You first.'

After a brief hesitation, Cassie took the pill from her sister's hand and swallowed it. It didn't feel like a day for control. It was in the air. Carnival.

***

By the time they got into town, Cassie's mood had lifted and lifted until she had reached a kind of warm euphoria. She'd even felt the urge to talk to the other carnival-bound people on the bus: the group of giggling pre-teen girls maybe on one of their first outings without parents, the guy holding what looked like an inflatable pirate, the group dressed up like medieval villagers. She looked at Alex's bright eyes darting this way and that, and something very much like love for her sister suddenly rushed over her. Yes, she was infuriating and self-obsessed and begrudged her everything, but she was hers. She was part of her.

The town today had the sense of normal life suspended. Time itself had been given the day off. Everywhere she looked there were explosions of bunting, and people dressed up, and the pubs were spilling out into the streets. There was the smell of candyfloss and toffee and burgers and frying onions all mixed together. Roads had been closed off to cars for the parade of floats to come by later, and the route was lined with stalls selling books or homemade food or second-hand crap or tombola tickets. There was a band playing somewhere – or maybe several bands; the air itself seemed full of music, and for the first time in a long time, Cassie wanted to dance – really dance. She turned to look at Alex, and she *was* dancing.

'Look at them, Cass – they're all having a good time. For the first time, all these people are actually just enjoying themselves.'

It was like yesterday had never happened. Maybe it hadn't. Maybe none of the past year had happened.

She walked alongside Alex, looking around her at the thronging people and the sky and the bunting and an escaped balloon flying free. Alex was examining the stalls as they went by. She stopped to admire some handmade jewellery, holding up a bright, chunky necklace that matched her dress, and asked the woman selling them – a woman around their age, probably called Rowan, wearing floaty scarves and what looked like a sackcloth skirt – how much it cost. She handed over the money and slipped it over her head immediately. A group of local guys, already full of booze, stared openly at the two of them, and Cassie stared back, secure in her bubble of chemical contentment and that something else – that Otherness, the sense that she had a dark secret – that set her apart from everyone else. One of them whistled, and Alex blew them a kiss.

'Witch! You have made a covenant with the devil and committed heinous acts of maleficium.'

The man who'd accosted her was wearing a tall hat and some kind of vaguely seventeenth-century garb, and he was pointing at her in a theatrical way, brows knitted together. She drew back.

'I can look on any witch and tell by her countenance what she is.'

'Can you?'

Alex giggled.

'Don't mind him, love,' said a woman standing near her – one of the ones in old-timey garb from the bus earlier. 'That's the historical reenactment society. That there's Matthew Hopkins, Witchfinder General. Or Simon, as he's normally called. Runs the grocer's shop down the road there. Mad all this, isn't it?'

'Do not address the witch,' said the tall man. 'I will prick thee and find out what—'

A few women rushed past in similar period dress, faces smeared with dirt. A couple of them had gone so far as to black their teeth out.

'There they go!' shouted someone excitedly. 'After them, Hopkins!'

The tall guy took off gamely in pursuit. By this point Alex had tears of laughter running down her face.

'Witch,' she said, pointing at Cassie.

'Whatever passes the time, I suppose.' Right now, her mood could not be soured.

'Don't worry,' said the woman next to her with a certain relish. 'He gets his comeuppance later – happens every year, sort of fete tradition. Later on you see, Hopkins gets put on trial and he's going to be dunked in the sea. It's all good fun.'

'Is that historically accurate?' muttered Cassie.

The woman shrugged. 'It's all good fun,' she repeated.

'He's got your number anyway,' muttered Alex in Cassie's ear.

They continued down the street. They were coming up to the church, where Grandad Maddon's body was buried while his soul – according to the words scratched on his grave marker – burned in Hell. There were more stalls here. Bric-a-brac and tombolas and homemade jams.

Alex clutched Cassie's arm. 'Look, Cass, it's Mrs Gibbett – oh God, she's seen us. We'll have to go over and say hello now. Do you think it's going to be odd after that grilling you gave her yesterday?'

'I didn't give her a grilling. Anyway, she was so pissed she probably won't remember.'

'Well, let's go and look at whatever it is she's flogging,' said Alex, and Cassie allowed herself to be dragged by the arm.

Mrs Gibbett was standing behind her stall of homemade knitted items – people and animals and flowers, hard to tell what any of it was really *for*. Was this what she did in her evenings on her own in that house? Anyway, she seemed delighted to see them.

'Enjoying yourselves, girls? My, look at you both; look at you, Cassie – don't you look fancy.'

Alex raised an eyebrow. 'Doesn't she?'

'Well, do you want to buy one? It's for a good cause, re-member – the church roof.'

'I'll have this,' said Alex abruptly, picking up a knitted orange starfish.

'Lovely; that'll be four pounds.'

She wrapped it up in a paper bag and handed it to Alex with a hand that, Cassie noticed with surprise, was shaking a little. *Not the DTs, surely, after one gin & tonic session?*

'Well, I'd better get on, but do enjoy yourselves today.'

'Oh, we couldn't do anything but.'

They headed back towards the town centre.

'Shall we go to the pub now?' said Alex. 'Joe said he'd meet me at the Crown at two. We can settle in for the afternoon.'

The sound of the band was getting closer; a parade of floats hovered into view. On the first one, a teenage girl was seated on what looked like a dining room chair festooned with toilet paper. Sitting on her own up there, a young girl surrounded by parading men and women in medieval fancy dress, she looked like a ritual sacrifice.

'Don't think much of the Carnival Queen,' muttered Alex. 'Is she wearing a tutu?'

'Don't be mean, she's only a kid.'

'Since when did you care about being mean? Anyway, we should have been the Carnival Queens, me and you.'

Alex spun around, and for a moment it looked very much like she was going to attempt to mount the float. Then her eyes lit up and she waved and shouted, 'Joe! JOE! You're just in time to miss the parade.'

He made his way easily through the crowd towards them, and then Alex grabbed him by the hands, spinning him around and nearly falling into the road. He laughed, steadying her, and then he turned to Cassie, and he couldn't, she thought, fail to notice that she was all dressed up. She smiled at him, for once not uncomfortable to feel his eyes on her, knowing that today she was beautiful.

But she wasn't prepared for the way he stared at her, all of her, his eyes travelling from her head down to her feet. It was probably only for a moment, but even the sounds around them – the music and the ritualistic floats and the band – faded into the background and it was just the two of them.

Then the moment was gone and the world came back.

'Hello,' he said. He turned to Alex, who was tugging at his arm.

'Come on,' she said. 'I've had enough of this. Are you coming with us, Cass?' She gestured to the pub down the road.

'I'll join you in a bit.'

'Alright. Goodbye, Ruby Tuesday.'

Alex dragged Joe into the crowd, and for a moment Cassie felt an unreasonable pang of loss. Then she shook it away because the sun was shining and the feeling of euphoria from Alex's pill had not let go of her yet. She closed her eyes, breathing in the warmth and the cotton-candy air. *Not today. Just one day away from it all.*

When she opened her eyes, she noticed a couple of guys next to her – good-looking in a nondescript way, probably only in their early twenties – and one of them smiled at her when she caught his eye. She smiled back. The music played and she let her body sway to it.

I will not be afraid. The sun is shining and I will not be afraid.

The music pounded inside and outside of her head. She moved further down the line of people along the street. The next float was filled with children dressed as sea creatures, with one of them as King Neptune in the middle, complete with plastic trident. As it passed close by her, a couple of children dressed as red crabs snapped their claws in her direction, and they seemed to grow, and then she was back on the beach again, throwing the box of claws into the sea, and when she looked around her for a moment, the town didn't look shiny and carnival-esque anymore. It was rotting. She could see discarded food on the ground, a dead bird lying in the road. Even the sky seemed to have darkened. She stepped backwards in alarm, right into one of the two guys who had smiled at her a few moments ago.

'God, I'm sorry.'

'You're more than welcome. Don't suppose you know a decent place to get a drink around here?'

He had a posh-boy voice and posh-boy hair and clothes. They looked like over-privileged students on a summer jolly to find out what the plebs did with their free time. The pub was clearly visible across the road, but she knew that what they really wanted was for her to go with them. Why not?

'I'm about to go over there to meet my sister; come with me if you like.'

She didn't ask their names; she didn't care. And so it was that when she entered the heaving pub in Lucie's green silk dress it was with her arms linked with two strangers. Alex and Joe had somehow managed to grab a table in the corner, so they joined them and settled in for what would turn out to be a long afternoon, while the carnival went on outside.

14

Posh Boys One and Two had just finished university, they said, and they were going from place to place for a few months. What had brought them here she couldn't figure out, unless they had just come to gawp at the locals. Didn't these types of people normally go and build huts in Africa before becoming investment bankers? Alex had dated a few of them in her time. Anyway, they had money and they bought drinks all afternoon and into the evening, and Alex flirted with them enthusiastically in the little time she had left from making Bambi eyes at Joe.

Cassie felt relaxed for the first time in months, or even years. She leaned back into her seat and luxuriated in the feel of her aunt's silk dress against her skin. She was overdressed for the pub – so was Alex – but she didn't care about that either. Later in the afternoon a '90s covers band had started up on a small stage in the corner and some people were dancing; Alex joined them for a while and the PBs watched her, admiring. Probably thinking, *Not bad for an old bird.*

She lost all track of time. She cadged fags off people like in the old days and smoked with abandon.

At some point during the afternoon – or was it early evening? – she led PB1 outside and kissed him in an alleyway among the empty beer barrels. His hands moved down her and she pushed them further down, impatient, all of a sudden, to feel. Anything. When she came back to the table, he bought another round of drinks and tried to talk to her about himself, or about herself, but any interest she'd had in him had gone.

At another point she heard shouts outside and looked out the window into the street to see Matthew Hopkins – Simon the Grocer – still bawling about witchcraft and devilry, being carted off on a chair for his dunking in the sea, surrounded by a mob of women, various puritanical-looking men and a parade of delighted kids.

It got later, and finally, her euphoria began to wear off – as of course she'd known it would, like Cinderella had known that the clock would eventually strike midnight – to be replaced by the familiar sensation of emptiness and life-as-it-was. With the kind of clarity that only comes when you've been drinking all day and you can't be drunk anymore, she thought that there was something *wrong*.

At about 11 p.m. or thereabouts, she got up to go to the toilet, leaving Alex laughing over some joke PB1 or PB2 had told – she couldn't tell if it was good or bad, didn't matter. She stood and stretched her arms, yawning, suddenly exhausted, then began the lengthy process of weaving through the tables and groups of people.

'Bloody Christ,' said a voice to the right of her.

She looked over at a guy walking back from the bar, balancing a tray of pints. He had a big red face and a big red nose and a haystack head of hair.

'I'm sorry, didn't mean to make you jump, but for a second there, I thought you were someone else.' His voice was loud, pissed.

'Who?'

'You're Lucie Maddon's niece, aren't you, from up the old house on the cliff? You scared the shit out of me – for a second I thought you was her. I did a bit of painting around the house for her a couple of times, you see.'

'I don't remember you.'

'No, don't suppose you would.' He leaned closer, swaying, his beery breath on her face now. 'She was a lovely woman, your aunt. I liked her a lot. A *lot*. Real lady that woman was. Kind you don't see much anymore, although...' And here he looked her up and down. 'You're a sight for sore eyes, too.'

The tray of pints was swaying dangerously now. She stepped back from him, and as she did he overbalanced and the tray of drinks smashed on the floor to the sound of cheers and laughter (some of it, she thought, coming from her dear sister). The guy muttered and bent down to try to salvage what couldn't be salvaged. The barman came over.

'Leave it, Tony, I'll sort it out. You alright, love?'

'I'm fine, don't worry about it.'

'OK, you have a nice night.'

'Sure. Thank you.'

Wanting to get out as quickly as possible, she pushed her way through the people to the double doors that led to the toilets and on the other side, she leant back against them for a moment, breathing deep. She caught sight of herself in a long mirror along the right wall, and for a second she was taken aback at the person she saw with the lipstick and the beautiful dress and the hooded eyes. She *was* like Lucie – and how had she never seen it until this moment? She smiled to herself, a secret smile of glee, but it quickly fell. Lucie... but did that mean she was like Bella, too? Because somewhere in Bella's face, hadn't there been the faint ghost of her mother, like an abortive version of the real thing? Pale blue eyes where Lucie's had been green; lank hair where Lucie's had curled.

'You need another cigarette,' she told her reflection, whoever she was, and her reflection nodded.

She pushed open the door to the beer garden and went to sit on the furthest bench, near the back wall. The sky was dark now, but the garden was illuminated with strings of lights. There were flies dancing around them, those particular kinds of night creatures you get in seaside towns. Behind the closed doors of the pub, she could still hear the muffled sounds of the band playing 'I Don't Want to Talk About It' by that guy who used to play with Neil Young and overdosed on heroin only everyone thought it was by Rod Stewart, and beyond that, the last dying sounds of the fete. Only one other table was occupied, near the door, by a man in a pirate hat who was singing along in a maudlin sort of way. She was just beginning to idly amuse herself by making up stories as to why this was when a shadow fell over the table. She turned around to see Joe.

'Mind if I join you for a smoke?' His face looked tired and pale.

She gestured to the seat opposite. 'Go ahead. Been quite a day, hasn't it?'

'I suppose so.'

Joe appeared on edge, she noticed, in a way she hadn't seen before. Usually, he was placid, calm – part of the background. Now he was like an incidental character in a film or a book who had fought his way to the front and didn't know what he was supposed to be doing there. He was shifting from side to side a little and he kept running one of his hands through his hair. Without thinking much about what she was at, she reached out to take it – to still it, but also because it was something she'd never done and she wanted to try it out. The hand was rough and warm, but dry. He looked up and their eyes met, then, very deliberately, he put his other hand out and brushed it down the side of her face. Instinctively, she closed her eyes and remembered that day on the beach again, all those years ago when she'd been on the cusp of life.

'Are you alright?'

She laughed a little because her heart – her stupid, fucked heart – had started to beat faster.

And Alex always says I don't have one.

'In what way?'

'You looked sad out here, when I came out, before you saw me. For the rest of the day, you've seemed more relaxed than usual, but now...'

'I didn't know you noticed.'

'I've noticed you ever since I came here.'

She hesitated. What the hell? 'But then, what about Alex?'

He didn't say anything for a moment; he watched a moth that was trying to go into the light. His next words were unexpected – seemingly apropos of nothing.

'Those guys you brought along with you – they're pricks. Over-privileged pricks.'

She shrugged, surprised. 'They're harmless, I guess; young and a bit dim. Anyway, I can't really dislike someone for that. Alex and I were sent to a private boarding school, remember?'

'You're different. You're part of the place.'

'Are we?'

'*You* are.'

She let go of his hand.

'Are you alright, Joe? You seem a bit...'

But then he gave himself a little tap on the side of the head, like a self-reprimand, and laughed in a rueful sort of way. 'Like you said, it's been a long day.'

They sat in silence for a moment, looking down at the table, each drawing on their cigarettes.

Then he said, 'Alex told me about the cat. I'm sorry. What happened?'

She felt like Lucie had just died, all over again. It was like being hit in the throat, and she almost choked on the cigarette and thought – with the horror of unfamiliarity – that her eyes might be welling up. It was the smoke, of course. She moved back from him a little, consciously drawing away.

'We don't know what happened. Age, maybe? Anyway, it's done now, and it's not like she was really *ours*. I never much liked cats, to tell you the truth, so you don't need to be sorry.'

'Jesus.'

'What?'

'Do you always throw sympathy back in people's faces?'

'I don't know. I don't mean to. Since Lucie, since my aunt...'

She stopped. It was the second time she'd surprised herself by letting her guard down around him.

But he took up her words – rescued them, before they fell to the floor and smashed like that tray of drinks. 'Since your aunt what?'

'It's nothing. It's being back here, I imagine.'

'Do you want to talk about it?'

She laughed again – a real laugh, this time. 'To you?'

'What's wrong with me?'

'There's nothing *wrong* with you.'

Her cigarette was burned out, but already she wanted another one. He could see, and he passed her his packet. She took one and lit it.

'Did that man upset you?'

'What man?'

'You know. The one in the pub who said you looked like your aunt and then fucked his drinks all over the floor.'

'Oh. Him. I didn't know any of you guys heard that part of it. No, he was just... he was just drunk, I guess. I think we all are.'

'I could always see there was a lot of history there.'

'Where?'

'With... with your aunt and her family, with everything.'

'Why do you say that?'

He shrugged. 'People talk, that's all. And I may look like a big ignorant man, but I'm observant enough in my own way, you know.'

She looked out across the pub garden, where the man at the table near the door had stopped singing to himself and was examining something near his foot. In the distance she could see the outline of the church with its crumbling roof and the scaffolding around it. Somewhere, further out towards the sea, there was a light.

'It did upset you, didn't it?'

Fucking hell. She looked back at him. 'And if it did, would that be strange?' she snapped. 'All these people all the time, whispering, insinuating, making assumptions about them.'

'Them?'

'My aunt and Bella. Come on, you know all about my cousin; everyone does. She was wrong and bad and all the rest of it. The Devil child.'

'I didn't really know her, to tell you the truth.'

'Well, if it hadn't been for her, Lucie would've... She'd have had a different kind of life. That's true enough.'

'Maybe she didn't want a different kind of life.'

'Oh, come on. Didn't want to? Did you never see her? She should have been in a – in the centre of a room full of beautiful people at a party. All her life. But instead, for some reason, she moved back to that house with that old bastard and produced our cousin and then stayed to bring her up, for all the joy that brought her. I suppose she thought Bella would be someone to love. Maybe she thought it would make up for losing... But what is it about that house that drags people in?'

Cassie realised she was talking more to herself now and she stopped, annoyed and puzzled. Must be more pissed than she realised. He was staring at her now, or rather, he wasn't looking at *her* – he was looking in her direction but also *through* her, like he was looking at the space where she sat but she wasn't in it.

She met his eyes. It was a habit, that, refusing to back down from a stare. She watched like she was someone else as he put out his hand to her face and traced it with his finger, all the way down her neck and to her shoulder, and she didn't think to stop him. She shivered, but she wasn't cold.

'I feel like I should tell you...' he began.

There was a crash from over near the back door of the pub. The guy in the pirate hat who had been leaning over to look at his shoe had overbalanced and taken the table with him. He lay sprawled on the floor like a tortoise on its back.

It was just a second, but it gave her time to remember, again, who she was – that she was Cassie who also wore a shell. She stood up and looked down at Joe, her legs suddenly weak. He was looking away at something else, his face sad, his hand still poised in mid-air to reach for her. She felt as though she wanted to hurt him – she wanted to hurt everybody. That she would be glad to inflict pain.

'People always say too much when they drink, have you noticed that? I'm tired now, Joe – I'm going back in.'

She turned and headed back into the pub, stepping over the struggling man-tortoise near the doorway, arms still wriggling but apparently not concerned that the world had turned upside down, just like that.

15

Back in the pub, the band had finally stopped and the juke-box was playing 'The Hounds of Love' by Kate Bush on low, probably Alex's choice. Alex herself was sitting in between the posh boys, whose contented faces now irritated Cassie beyond all sense or reason. She felt as though all eyes were on her, judging, wondering what she'd been up to. After putting her arm up to the others at the table in acknowl-edgement, she bypassed it and went to look out of the win-dow, through a gap in the closed, mud-coloured curtains. A group of people were staggering past with bottles of cider. The Carnival Queen, off the float now but still wearing her tiara, had her gown tucked up in her knickers and what looked like vomit down her tulle cleavage. She was being held upright by a friend. Beyond that, in the town square, a couple were kissing. Everywhere, the detritus of the day's festivities lay scattered – discarded wrappers, burgers, bunting – like the smouldering remains of an explosion. Someone, somewhere, was singing.

She watched the Carnival Queen and her friends until they were out of sight at the end of the high street. She saw them turn the corner and then, right where they'd been, there was a figure, looking back at her. She turned away from it because it had no right to be here.

The tingling in her fingers was back with a vengeance after leaving her alone all day. It was starting to move up her arms. Shouldn't have had that pill, shouldn't have smoked, shouldn't have drunk so much. Shouldn't have done a lot of things. She turned back to the room. *Time to leave. If Alex isn't going, I'll go on my own.*

There were still plenty of people in the pub, but it felt quieter, somehow. More subdued. A group of older guys was sitting in the corner with pints, making muttered conversation. There were some others at the bar finishing their drinks and talking to the landlord about nothing in particular. Maybe it was the ringing in her ears, but she felt that they were talking so quietly they were almost miming; it took her to a different place from the rest of them. It took her to a secret world where people were making gestures with their hands but their eyes were saying different things. She went over to the table where Alex and the others were sitting. They looked up, like they'd been waiting for her. She was about to announce her intention to leave when Posh Boy One said, 'There you are. Time for shots before they kick us out? I'm buying.'

One more wouldn't hurt. But were they expecting to come back with her and Alex to the house afterwards? They were in for a disappointment, if so. Or a fortunate escape, depending on how you viewed it.

She yawned. 'OK,' she said, but didn't sit down with them. Instead, she stood over the table, watching them all, feeling the room spinning like a slow carousel and part of her, perversely, liking the effect she must be having in Lucie's green dress.

She saw Alex staring up at her. 'Sit down then, Cass,' she said, and then her eyes flickered past her, and Cassie knew that Joe must have come back in the room.

'There you are, my man,' said Posh Boy One.

Tomorrow he would wake up and the two of them would carry on their ironic tour of rural England and they'd go home and sit in a wine bar or a private members' club and tell Bertie and Clementine and Rupert stories about the funny little happening in the kooky seaside town. And possibly about the birds they'd happened upon there who were getting on a bit but weren't half bad for their age. They were harmless enough, though. Just kids.

She was looking at him, musing on this, as he passed Joe on his way to the bar. She saw him jerk his head in her direction and say, in what was no doubt supposed to be an all-boys-together *sotto voce*, only he clearly wasn't used to speaking in a low voice:

'Tell you what, if there was another one like her in the green dress, I'd like to meet her; maybe a few years younger though. Not really much talent going on around here, is there?'

She winced. As soon as she'd had this last shot, it really was time to leave.

It all happened very quickly. One moment she was standing there, bored, restless, wanting to leave; the next, Joe had launched himself at Posh Boy One and he was on the ground. Alex had jumped up from her chair just in time to avoid them crashing into her. For a while – a long while, it seemed, although it could only have been seconds – all Cassie could hear was the sound of fists meeting flesh and bone. Either Joe was too strong or the boy was too pissed to help himself, she didn't know. Posh Boy Two seemed frozen to the spot, just like she was in these first few moments, and then there was the sound of a bottle smashing and Joe had picked up the jagged stump, and Alex was next to her and someone screamed.

That's when it seemed the rest of the pub unfroze. Finally, a few guys from around the bar got Joe and dragged him away from the boy. When they pulled him up, Joe's face wasn't his face anymore; he looked dazed and his eyes were blank.

She looked down at the bloody mess that was the boy's face and then looked away as something rose in her stomach. She put her hand on the side of the table and took deep breaths, steadying herself. Next to her, she heard Alex whisper, 'Oh God, look at him'.

The music was still going on the jukebox; it was playing 'Groove Is in the Heart', by Deelite.

The men were still holding on to Joe, but awkwardly now, like someone had given him them to hold and wandered off and now they didn't quite know what to do with him. Joe wasn't struggling though; he was saying, 'I'm sorry,

I'm sorry,' over and over, and the landlord had come out from behind the bar and he was kneeling down next to Posh Boy One; now Posh Boy Two was kneeling down too and saying, 'You'll be alright, you'll be alright,' over and over and again, only what did *he* know?

'Keep hold of him,' said the barman. 'The police are on their way.'

But then, with a sudden lunge, Joe twisted himself free and made for the door, and before anyone could even register what was happening, he was gone. Someone half-heartedly made chase in the dark, but they soon came back, panting and leaning over and coughing up phlegm. Not long after that, they heard the police sirens.

Cassie looked down at the barely conscious boy on the ground. She became aware of Alex standing beside her and she turned to look at her properly. She was pale, and for once, completely silent. She looked Cassie straight in the eyes in what seemed to be an accusing way, and the thought came to her: *She blames this on me. Of course she does. It's always my fault.*

The ambulance came and took the boys away. The police stayed to ask questions, but it was over mercifully quickly, a simple case of one too many mixed with volatile tempers – that was what they were going to put it down to, she could tell already, and why not? It was as good an explanation as any.

A small, dark-haired policewoman questioned her and Alex and took their contact details. They told the woman all they knew about Joe, which – when it came down to it – wasn't much at all.

'So you say he's not a close friend of yours?'

'No. We've only been here a few weeks.'

'Well, if he tries to contact you, I want you to inform us right away. He could be dangerous.'

Cassie thought about that. Dangerous. What did that even mean?

The police strongly hinted they'd all had enough excitement for one night, and one by one the punters left. The last bus had gone hours ago, of course, and there was no Joe to give them a lift home.

'Shall we try to get hold of one of the local cab firms, if there are any?' said Cassie.

'No,' said Alex. It was the first word she'd spoken to Cassie since it all happened. 'No. I'd rather just walk.'

'That'll take a couple of hours.'

'I don't care.'

Neither did Cassie, she realised, as long as she wasn't here. They left.

Somewhere between her last cigarette and now, the night had got cold and the town had got silent. They walked through the scattered remains of the carnival, down the main street and on and on towards the coast road. On the way they passed the man-tortoise crawling home. The sky was an endless blanket of stars.

16

They barely spoke on the way back, and once they had left the town behind them, the silence became like a third person walking alongside them. It was a clear night, so their way was lit by the stars and the almost-full moon – just as well, because there were no streetlights on this lonely stretch of road that edged the coast like a ribbon. As there was no pavement, they walked in the middle of the road. There was no traffic at this time of night, and if the odd car did come along, they could hear and see it coming a mile off.

A couple of times during the long, long walk, she looked over at Alex. Her face was still a pale blank and she stared straight ahead, so Cassie didn't try to talk about it either. The silence suited her. Her arms and legs were weights pulling her down to the earth with each step. If she lay down now on the road, she knew she could have fallen asleep forever.

She tried not to think of the boy's face, pummelled and obliterated until it looked more like something that might hang in a butcher's shop than the collection of features that had been pressed up so close to hers earlier that evening. *Do I make all these things happen? Lucie? Bella? The boy? Joe?*

She could see the dark, waiting shape of the cliff house ahead of them, long before they reached it. But as they got closer, she noticed there was also a light a little further down the road, coming from Mrs Gibbett's house. She looked at her phone and saw it was just coming up to 3 a.m. Soon the dawn would begin.

The light was coming from the woman's sitting room and there was the sound of Mozart playing, familiar from her years with Lucie but somewhat out of place in what she assumed to be Mrs Gibbett's prosaic world. The curtains were not quite drawn, and she caught movement behind them and a swish of bright colour. She glanced at Alex to see if she'd registered the oddity of this too, but either she hadn't noticed or she didn't care.

'Weird time for her to be up,' Cassie muttered, but her sister still said nothing and marched on ahead up to the house.

Without pausing to question why she was doing it, Cassie moved closer to the window where there was a chink in the curtains. The woman was sitting in an armchair with a glass in her hand, wearing one of Lucie's shawls. It was one Lucie had brought back from Morocco and hung on the wall of her bedroom, and she'd told them stories about what it was like to be there as Cassie stroked the colourful fabric.

She's waiting for Lucie, even though Lucie isn't coming back.

The woman turned towards the window, and Cassie drew back, leaning against the side of the house for a moment to catch her breath, her heart beating fast. Then she hurried up the long driveway after Alex, through the kitchen door and into the dark hallway, where the sound of the clock ticking was louder than it had ever been.

Cassie had expected Alex to go straight up to bed, but when she went into the living room, she was sitting at Lucie's piano, idly picking notes out.

'Are you not going to bed after all that?'

Alex said nothing; she stared straight in front of her.

'You've barely said anything the whole way home. Look, Al, what happened earlier was terrible but you didn't really know anything about Joe, did you? You couldn't have known that he'd—'

'Fuck Joe,' said Alex.

'What?'

'I said fuck Joe. Fuck you too, Cassie.'

Now Alex turned away from the piano to face her, but in the semi-darkness it was hard to read her expression.

'I'm sorry?'

Cassie was tired – beyond tired. She told herself she didn't have the time or energy for her sister's petulance. She couldn't reason with her now.

She turned to walk towards the stairs. 'Look, I'm going to bed, Alex. If you're somehow blaming me for—'

There was a crash of discordant notes.

'I saw you with him.'

'With who?'

She thought of the boy with his hands all over her, only now when she pictured his young face pressed close to her, it was bloody and mangled and the blood was seeping into her mouth and it tasted both metallic and sweet. The reverberations from the piano still hung in the air.

'With Joe. I was coming out for a smoke, but then I saw you sitting outside and I saw you together...' Alex's voice was hard, but Cassie could see her holding her arms to her chest, like she was giving herself a hug because other people wouldn't. Couldn't.

'I don't know what you thought you saw, but God...'

'Just because I was getting close to him and he liked me, and you – you don't even *have* any feelings.'

'What does that mean?'

Cassie switched on the lamp next to the door and moved further into the room. In the sudden light she could see that Alex's enormous eyes were puffy, red, streaked with mascara. She looked like a child playing dress-up.

'It's all secrets with you, isn't it? Secrets, secrets, secrets. Cassie will never let anyone close to her unless she feels like it. I'm tired of trying. All these weeks we've been here; all these years, actually.'

'Trying? Come on, Alex – all you ever do is try to wind me up. It's all some kind of competition with you. Anyway, it's nearly dawn. Can't we just talk about this tomorrow when you're calmer?'

'But I know about you. Everyone says, "Oh, isn't Cassie like Lucie?" You're nothing like her really – I was the one who understood her. She was – she was... You're more like Bella, I think. You have the same eyes, sometimes, when you look at people, and you don't really care about anyone and you rip things apart just for the sake of it. Like her.'

And Cassie thought, that's what's haunting us in this family: hate. Hate and the past. She clenched and flexed her burning hands. She looked down at them. Crab claws.

In the corner of her eye, she knew – she *knew* – that something had been there watching them, only it had scuttled away into the shadows as soon as she turned her head.

She took a breath, forcing herself to be calm, to be nothing, like she always was. Now she met her sister's huge eyes, waiting eagerly – almost too eagerly – for her to respond, to push back, and she had a sudden urge to give her a hug but she pushed it down. Instead, she said:

'You're such a baby.'

'That's all you have to say? And what about Joe?'

'*What about Joe?*'

She paused and glanced across at herself in the mirror over the fireplace, and this time she saw a broken, tired ghost of Lucie in her green dress, mascara smudged under her eyes. She looked away from the sight of this Other Lucie, nauseated.

'Yes, I know now that he's clearly bad news and all that – I really pick them, don't I? Alex picked another bad one, you can go ahead and say it. But you didn't know that earlier when you were all set to climb on each other.'

'Oh, listen, this is ridiculous; I'm going to bed. If you really want to know, Joe came up to me while I was sitting there on my own. I don't know why. Maybe it's because I'm not a needy woman-child with abandonment issues. Waiting for Daddy to come and save her.'

Why do I want to hurt people? Is it because it's easier?

She turned towards the stairs but lost her balance slightly and caught her toe on the side of the door. The pain pulsated through her foot and it made her angrier.

'Something's happening to you, isn't it?'

Cassie stopped and closed her eyes at the words, and suddenly the pain wasn't in her foot anymore. She opened them and looked down at the floor, at a faint mark on one of the boards. It had been there, she thought, ever since they'd been kids. Bella had been hurt; she'd hurt herself somehow. She'd cut her arm. Or maybe, after all, it was from when Cassie had cut herself the other week and her blood had dripped on the floor.

'All these secrets, Cassie, like I said. But you're struggling, I can see it – and don't think I don't remember before, all those years ago when we were kids, when they took you away after Bella died. Remember?'

'Shut up, Alex.'

'I've seen the way you drink so you don't have to think about it, whatever it is – oh, I know I'm not one to talk, but you can't stop. You make out you're so in control, but I think you're sick – really sick. You think I don't see things – Alex doesn't see anything. But I do. I see things. I see that you take pills. What is it? What have you got?'

'Shut up, Alex. You don't know anything about anything.'

The pain in her toe had travelled up her body and it was a white-hot rage now. Alex didn't understand. It had been nothing – nothing, that time all those years ago. Just a blip. A misunderstanding. All those people in white coats trying to get her to *talk* as though they thought they knew more than her, and the garden that was supposed to be soothing, and those other stupid, stupid kids.

Now she looked up and took a breath before talking again.

'All this is because Lucie liked me best, isn't it, Al? Jealousy eats you up, doesn't it? Oh, she was fond of you, of course. Probably thought you were silly – prone to doing silly things – not as much trouble as Bella, obviously, but still. Maybe that's how it was with all of them. Dad, even Mum, before she topped herself – but of course, you're probably too young to even remember her. I remember her – that's something else Lucie and I had. And why are you sitting at the piano? You can't even play it.'

She waited for the tears to come, for Alex to fly at her, even, to scratch at her eyes or rip her skin off her rotten bones bit by bit and pull her to pieces. She wanted her to. *My body is my crumbling temple.*

But Alex didn't do any of that. She stood still, for a long moment, staring at her with wide, wondering eyes. And then, in a steady, toneless voice, she said:

'Have her. Have Lucie all to yourself, or what's left of her. Have them all – I'm going back home. I should never have come here. But you'll be sorry, Cass. What's sad is that I actually came here to spend time with you – but you don't want that. You don't want me around.'

She brushed past Cassie on her way to the door, delicate beaded sandals swinging from her fingertips, toe rings tapping on the floor. Cassie heard little elven footsteps on the stairs, and then, with great finality, a door slamming.

She realised she had been holding her breath, and now she let it out in a shuddering wave. Her head dropped forward for a moment, as though that one held breath had been the only thing keeping her together. Was this what winning felt like?

Then, slowly, she lifted her head again and confronted the eyes in the mirror opposite her.

'Was that really necessary?' she muttered softly.

She went out into the hallway, looking up the stairs after Alex, listening for something, willing something to be there, waiting for her. Because if there really was something there, that meant this other stuff... *Do I want the house to be haunted? Do I want these things in the corners of my eyes to be real?*

Was a real haunting preferable to an imagined one? Someone had told her once that being afraid of something was far worse than the thing itself; but of course, being a person who wasn't afraid of so very much, she hadn't understood what they meant. Now maybe she did.

'If you're listening, Bella, I'm *glad* you're dead, do you hear?' she said.

Nothing. Silence.

The clock struck three and she was finally, finally alone. Just the ticking and, outside, the beginnings of the dawn chorus. She went back and sat at the piano and tried to pick out the notes of the *Moonlight Sonata*, only her fingers had seized up and her hand still throbbed where she had cut it, and the more she tried, the more panicked she became and her eyes glazed over until her fingers were pale blurs.

'Cassie?'

She whipped her head around to see a figure standing behind her. She blinked, but this time it was still there; this time there was something real. Joe had come back after all.

17

She woke to a glaring, belligerent sun. Blinking, she stretched and reached for her phone. 11 a.m. For a moment, she lay in the space between sleep and wakefulness. The cat... The carnival... The pub... That boy... Joe...

Something stirred beside her in the bed, and she turned her head to see him lying next to her, still asleep, one arm slung over his head. Then he turned over on his side and she saw raw claw marks on his back, like something had been trying to rip him to shreds. She looked down at her own fingers. Blood and skin were clagged under her nails. She was sore, she realised, and sick to the stomach; she'd drunk more yesterday than she would care to imagine. Her head was pounding and pounding like someone was hammering on the outside of it, like somebody or something wanted to get in. She felt – violated. She was naked, and on the floor next to the bed, Lucie's green dress was cast off like a snake-skin. When she sat up slowly and looked in the big mirror across from the bed, all she could see was herself again.

The mirror. That's when it hit her; they were in Lucie's room – in Lucie's bed. She got up too quickly; her right leg, still numb from sleep, gave way and she hit the floor, feeling a jarring pain in her arm. She swore, rubbing it, but none of this woke Joe from his dead-man slumber. She pulled herself up and padded across to the landing, the boards under her bare feet warmed by the sun.

Alex. Her sister's bedroom door was wide open but she wasn't in there. The room looked tidier than she'd ever seen it; Alex had even made the bed, as though in some last act of anti-defiance. Had she come in and seen Joe with Cassie this morning? Had she heard?

'Have Lucie all to yourself. Have them all.'

She went into her own room, pulled on a pair of jeans and a T-shirt and made her way slowly down the stairs, holding on to the banister, not trusting her shaking legs to hold her up on their own against the spinning and the nausea. Downstairs, she managed to make tea and perched at the end of the long kitchen table. There was no scratching today. There were no flashes in the corner of her eye. The place outside on the driveway where Alex's car had been parked was empty.

There was a knock at the door and it caused her hand to jerk, spilling hot tea over her bone-white wrist.

'Fuck,' she said.

She brushed her hair back with her hands, pulled herself up and went to the door; it was Mrs Gibbett, looking concerned. Beyond her, the day was almost offensive in its brightness, but even so the woman was wearing her standard wellingtons and heavy, grey jumper. Cassie's mind went back to how she had looked last night in Lucie's light, colourful shawl – had that even been real? – and her hand went to her throat. The woman was *wrong*.

'Hello, my dear. I just thought I should come to see if you were alright after... Goodness, you do look pale, and I can see your sister's car has gone. Is she...?'

'I'm fine, thank you. Did you make a lot of money yesterday for the church?'

'I heard about what happened – later.'

Of course she did; the woman knew everything. Everything. There was a familiar smell in the air – like jasmine mixed with something else – and it added to the nausea Cassie was already feeling.

She glanced up at the ceiling, involuntarily. 'It wasn't... I think people had drunk too much, that's all.'

She leaned against the doorway, deliberately holding her arm against it to stop the woman entering.

'Awful business, after such a lovely day too. And he's gone off, they say? The police are looking for him, of course.'

'Joe, you mean?'

'I always knew he was a bad lot back in the day, you see. I didn't like to say anything to either of you at the time; it wasn't my place, and your sister seemed quite taken with him, and I thought, well, he's older now, he's been away a time. I was always told you should give people the benefit of the doubt.'

Her face was expectant. Cassie knew she wanted to be invited in, to drink tea and share more confidences and continue to insinuate herself further, further into their lives.

'It's alright – it's all alright.'

Oh God, the nausea. Any second now she was going to fall on the floor. But Mrs Gibbett went on. She leaned forward slightly, and Cassie shrank back, not caring if the woman noticed her obvious repulsion.

'Perhaps I shouldn't have said anything.'

'You didn't really say anything,' said Cassie. 'But it doesn't matter.'

'Are you alright, my dear? You look a bit peaky. Few too many drinks last night after all, was it? Shall I come in and – is there anything I can do? I'm good when people are sick.'

She reached out her hand, and Cassie recoiled at the sight of her stubby fingernails. Again, they were flecked with bright red like they'd been painted recently and it had been badly removed. And then it occurred to her: Lucie used to paint her nails that deep, dark blood-red. And then she realised what the lingering smell was – how could she not have recalled it before? It was the perfume Lucie had always worn.

She's being nice but really she wants us out of here because she wants Lucie and this place all to herself – that's it, isn't it?

'I'm fine, really. It was a long day yesterday, as you say. I think I might go for some fresh air soon – go for a walk, you know.'

'I only care, you see.'

'I know, thank you – but you must have things to do.'

'Well, you're right there… No rest for the wicked, as they say. Take care of yourself then, Cassandra.'

'You too.' She managed to put a firm goodbye into her tone.

Cassie watched the woman tread back down the driveway to her lonely little house. Then she turned back to the kitchen table, to her cooling cup of tea. But suddenly the walls seemed to be closing in on her, threatening to suffocate, whispering things she didn't want to hear, so she went back up the stairs to wake Joe and tell him he had to leave, right now, because they'd find him. Only, when she opened Lucie's bedroom door, Joe was already sitting up in bed. He was holding Lucie's dress to his face and crying like she'd never seen anyone cry before. She stood there and watched him, and in that time she felt nothing but saw everything, while he scarcely seemed to see her at all. She may as well have been a ghost.

Eventually, after who knew how much time had gone by, he looked up and their eyes met.

'I think it still smells like her,' he said. 'Is that possible?'

We all loved Lucie, of course. Probably everyone who went near Lucie loved her. She steadied herself against the wall.

'*This* is why you came here? For Lucie? How come I never saw it?'

Joe's eyes were bloodshot and his face was pale. Yes, he was handsome, in his way, but he was not for her or even for Alex. She could feel her heart pounding like it wanted to leap out of her body, and for a moment it gave her strength.

'You have to go now, Joe, before I call the police.'

But again, he wasn't even looking *at* her but *through* her, and that's when it really hit her – he had been looking at someone else the whole time.

Then she looked up at the mirror hanging on the wall, and for a second she saw her again, too, saw her eyes and the proud tilt of her chin, and it frightened her. She almost put her hand out to reach out to her, to Lucie, to ask her who she had been, but then behind her – behind all that – there was someone else who looked at her with reproachful hate in her pale eyes. And behind them all it was still her, and she was all three of them. And then she put her hand down, and the figure in the mirror was only her again: just Cassie, pale and a little cracked. A broken imitation.

'You look so much like her,' Joe said. 'I saw it as soon as I got here. To start with, I just wanted to come back to – to see her house. I didn't mean to...'

'Did you... did you have some kind of *fixation* with Lucie all those years ago? Is that it?'

She wasn't prepared for the sudden change of mood, the flash of anger like in the pub last night. His right fist hit the bed.

'It wasn't just in my head if that's what you're thinking; we had something – it was special. You were just a kid back then, and you don't know how lonely she was. She had no one here, and there was no one like her. She shouldn't have been here at all – it was wrong for her to be here. When I came here with my Dad, I hardly dared talk to her for a long time, but then we were in the house on our own one day and... And she asked me about myself – first person who'd ever really taken an interest in *me* and what I wanted – then it led on from there. She... When she spoke to you, it made you feel like you were the only person worth talking to, like someone was shining a torch on you. She made me want to be better.'

Yes, that was true.

'But then I think that daughter of hers could sense what was between us too, even though we were careful; the way that girl used to look at me.' He shook his head.

Cassie couldn't tell if he was talking to her or to himself. Her ears were ringing.

'I was going to take her away from here, after her daughter disappeared – drowned herself, whatever – who really knows what happened? People around here used to say stuff, I know. They always talked. Lucie must have felt like she was living in some kind of glass bowl. I told her we had to take our chance now and go away from all of it, and I know she wanted to come with me – she *must* have wanted to.'

'But she didn't?'

He breathed heavily now, and she could see he was fighting back tears, and that was the worst thing. Instinctively, she stepped back.

'When I came to talk it through with her, she laughed at me and said I was just a kid. She told me to go away on my own and get on with my life – *have* a life was what she said. I was...'

'So that's when you left?'

'I should never have left, but I was so – hurt and angry. But I thought about her all the bloody time and I tried to make myself better. Pathetic, isn't it? I was making myself better so I could come back and she'd see I wasn't just a kid... Then I heard that she'd died and it was too late...'

The words floated somewhere above Cassie's head, and then she was being pulled down into unconsciousness. Pinpricks danced on the ceiling like the little specks of dust that dance in the dapples of sunlight, the ones Alex used to believe were fairies. And I-know-better Cassie, saying, *'They're not fairies, Alex. Things like that don't exist. None of that kind of thing is real.'* She closed her eyes and leaned her head on the doorframe so she didn't have to see his face anymore.

'Cassie?' he was saying. 'Cassie? Listen, you can come away with me instead. It's not too late for you.'

Then she opened her eyes, and the world was clear again.

'I'm not Lucie.'

'I'm serious; come with me now. There's nothing for you here either. We could start again together. Forget everything.'

'Get out while you've still got time, and never come back. I'm only saying this once.' She heard her voice and she didn't know how it sounded so calm, because she wasn't calm on the inside. On the inside she was a collapsing edifice of burning synapses, missing connections. 'If you don't, we'll kill you.'

He came towards her, reached out for her, so close that his heavy breath was in her face, sour from yesterday's drink, and she wondered how she could have ever... She wanted to scrape him out from underneath her fingernails.

She stepped back from him, away from the doorframe.

'You're wrong about her, you know. Whatever you felt for her – to Lucie, you would have been a distraction, that's all, like a toy. Do you really think *she* would have loved someone like you?'

'That's not...'

'I'm going now, and when I get back you'll be gone.'

She turned away.

'Wait...'

There was such a sudden urgency in his voice that she paused in spite of herself.

'What?'

'I have to tell you something else. *Please*. I wanted to tell you yesterday; I have to tell someone or it'll drive me crazy. It's this place, you know, it ate away at her. But it was that daughter of hers that was the *real* problem. Like I said, she saw – somehow she knew about me and Lucie, and I could tell that she hated me. We were so careful, the two of us, but there was one day she came suddenly into the bedroom and she saw us together. *It was her fault it all fell apart.*'

'You're blaming your problems on a disturbed child now?'

'She wasn't a real child. There was something wrong with her, you know that – everyone knew that. She didn't want Lucie to have anything or anyone. And now it eats away at me too, because...' He paused for a moment.

'Because what?'

'It's because of – that day. When she came in and saw us, Lucie told me to go and leave them together, and I've never seen two people look at each other that way, so I did leave. I wish I hadn't, I really do.'

For a second, the whole room darkened as Cassie *saw* it. She saw Lucie and Bella facing each other, trapped in their cage of hate and resentment and duty.

'What did Lucie do?'

'It was in winter, and God, it was so cold that year – you never came here in winter, so you don't know what it was like with that wind eating into you. For you it was all summers and swimming. I went out and I could hear this sound from upstairs – coming from the girl, I think it was, because it was like screaming but it didn't sound human. I went down to that old beach hut – you know the one – because that's where Lucie and I used to meet up sometimes. I thought – maybe she'd know and come and find me eventually, when it was all over, to tell me it was alright. But I watched the house for hours and nobody came out at all. Then that woman... that weird woman from down the road went in.'

'Mrs Gibbett?'

'She must have known too, all the time, about me and Lucie, because it seemed like she knew everything. She always – looked down on me, I think. Like I wasn't good enough. Like she was anything. She was always around though – you know, I think she had some kind of weird obsession with Lucie.'

'And what then?'

'Then nothing. It got darker and eventually, I left, so I don't know what happened next. It was later I heard that that girl had run away in the night and people said she'd drowned herself in the sea, and it didn't surprise me because she was... the way she was. But I thought – I thought if I'd stayed there, I'd have seen her come out and I could have stopped her, could have saved her even, so perhaps it was my fault too. But then I asked myself, I asked myself – *would* I have done?' He pressed his hand to his forehead. 'Anyway, it's stupid but part of me all this time never believed she went into the sea. Sometimes I think she's just still out there somewhere, waiting to get me back.'

'Not just you,' said Cassie softly.

'What?'

'Nothing – it's nothing.'

'So after that day, if I tried to get near Lucie, she pushed me away like I'd never been anything to her.' He gave a bitter laugh. 'Before my mum died, she told me that Lucie had left here and I thought, good. I thought maybe she'd even come to find me – stupid I know. Then I find out that, after everything, she'd ended up back here again – in this place of all places – just to die on her own. Like in the end she couldn't keep away – like there was some kind of string attached to her pulling her back here.'

Yes. Invisible hands, patiently pulling bit by bit.

His voice was low now, and she had to lean forward to hear what he was saying.

'I think I knew what it was – how it was with her and your cousin – but I did nothing because I loved her and it wasn't her fault. Oh God, but I think I knew.'

'Knew *what*?'

Cassie leaned on the doorframe, letting the words wash over her and half taking them in, remembering Bella's hands reaching out to her throat, that day in the attic. And then those unseen hands that had held her down in the bath; the hard, brutal voice she'd heard in her head as she'd lain there. All jumbled up together in her mind. *At the end of the day, people treat other people the way they've been treated. It's all they know.* Things were falling into place, but she didn't want them to, so she very deliberately pushed them away.

'Don't you be pulled in too, like her. Come away with me. I mean it – we can start again.'

She looked up again at the Lucie-her reflected back at her in the glass.

'We don't want to see you ever again,' she said. 'You don't *matter* anymore.'

With one movement, before she knew what she was doing, she grabbed the crumbling bust of the woman sitting on the mantelpiece and threw it as hard as she could at the mirror, which smashed into a million refracting pieces. Then she stood there, shaking, for a long, long moment, as the broken pieces of Lucie flashed all around her. She turned to Joe.

And then the world went – dark. Like being put under an anaesthetic; one second they're counting you down and the next a stranger is waking you up and a part of you has been removed, or altered.

18

The next thing Cassie knew she was on the shoreline. She fell on her knees on the sand and threw up until she felt there could be nothing conceivably left of all this inside her. She sat up, shaking, and wiped her mouth with her hand. Then she looked down at the pool of vomit mixed with seawater in front of her and saw there was blood. There was blood on her hands, too.

The washed-up whale had been taken away, but she felt there were still traces of it all around her.

'Are you alright, love? Get away from there, you.'

Still shaking with the effort of retching, she looked up at the man standing over her. A large, shaggy dog, seawater dripping from its fur, was sniffing around her feet and had begun to lick at the pool of vomit in front of her. In amongst it there were shells and crab claws, and had they come from out of her or had they been there already? And what was wrong with this guy? Could he not *see* the blood on her and on the sand? Her stomach churned again, but she pulled herself to her feet.

'I'm fine now, thank you,' she said shortly, hanging on to the last, splitting threads of control.

The sun was glittering on the sea. It was a beautiful day.

'You look like you need a lie down. You're from the house up there, aren't you? Fancied a bit of fresh air, did you? I know how you feel, love, when I used to...'

The guy carried on talking, but she wasn't listening. Something had caught her eye near the rotting beach hut in the distance. She got up, leaving him mid-sentence.

'Oh, off are you? Don't mind me.'

She only half-registered his annoyance at her rudeness. She made her way towards the figure she knew she'd seen – the sand under her feet alternately hot and damp depending on how close she walked to the shoreline. But like Alice in the looking-glass world with the Red Queen, however fast she went, the further away the hut and the figure seemed to get. The sand made her legs heavier and heavier and a seagull shrieked overhead like it was warning her off, but she kept going, kept moving, as though somehow reaching the figure now was the most important thing in the world.

'Bella!' she called out. 'I know.'

But when she finally reached the hut, there was nobody standing outside it. She made for the doorway in case the figure – *she* – had gone in there for shelter (*From what, Cassie? The sun? The dead don't mind the sun.*) but the stench that greeted her when she got close was appalling, even worse than the whale on the beach. She didn't look inside.

This was where Lucie and Joe had met sometimes. A nauseating picture appeared in her mind of them, in here, bodies locked together among the rotting timbers. Who was Lucie?

Who am I? What's happening to me?

She sank down on the sand, defeated, legs numb, then she lay on her back and stared up at the sky, which was speckled with tiny scuds of white clouds. She took a few deep breaths, like they'd told her to do, and tried to ignore the tingling creeping up her body and towards her brain. Slowly, slowly it comes again...

Then a shadow fell over her. She sat up and span around, scrabbling backwards on the sand with her burning fingers in a sudden, irrational panic.

'I didn't mean to frighten you. I saw you come out. You're all on your own now.'

She looked up, shading her eyes from the sun. It was that girl – Billie – holding the doll over her shoulder, standing there looking down at her with a solemn expression on her face, her eyes wide and green and flecked with little bits of brown in the middle. She was so still, it was almost as though she wasn't a person at all but a figure somebody had carved and planted in the sand. The scarred, broken part of her face looked sore today – raw, as though she'd been out in the sun too much and hadn't put cream on it.

'You didn't frighten me,' she lied.

What the girl said next was unexpected.

'It wasn't me that killed the orange cat, you know.'

Cassie laughed, in spite of herself, in spite of the fact that there was nothing to really laugh about.

'I know that – I know.' Although she hadn't, because who could be sure of anything anymore?

The girl nodded.

'You're kind, really,' she said.

A wave of shame came over Cassie, because she knew that whatever she was – whatever she had been in her life – she wasn't kind. She was like one of Bella's crab shells, brittle on the outside and empty and rotted away underneath. That's what she was.

'I'm not – I'm not. I'm sorry, Billie – I'm so sorry about what happened to you all those years ago. I should have stopped it – I should have warned you. I should have *done* something. My cousin... I'm sorry. I knew what was, we all knew what she was and I didn't do anything.'

The girl shook her head, cutting her off. 'You should go away now, before it's too late. They'll want you to stay, but you can't.'

'Too late for what?'

'She's bad. I saw it then and I see it now. I see lots of things.'

Cassie took a deep breath. 'Look, Bella's gone now, Billie, and she can't hurt you. Everyone's gone now, in fact, if it comes to that. It's just me.'

Billie shook her head and dropped her voice.

'People all say I'm daft and broken like her.' She stroked the doll's head tenderly. 'But I see everything. And I don't mean her. I mean the other one.'

And out there in the beating sun, skin exposed and forehead still clammy after the sickness, Cassie felt a cold ice-pick work its way down her spine.

'The other one?'

'You know.'

And yes, she did know – maybe somehow, deep down, she had always known.

The dog was back again, sniffing around Cassie's feet. Billie leapt backwards and the doll fell from her arms. Just before she bent down to pick it up, Cassie saw that the part of its face that had been cracked was now almost gone entirely; there was just one eye and then a gaping hole.

'Sorry, love, I keep running into you, don't I?'

The guy from further down the beach was standing a few feet away from her, a half-smile on his face.

'Yes.'

'Don't worry, I can see you don't want to talk. Nice day and all that. Come here, you.' He whistled the dog away and carried on up the beach.

Flustered at the interruption, Cassie turned back to Billie only to find she had already gone. She saw a hurriedly retreating figure up on the sand dunes that might have been her, if a person could move that fast. In any case, she knew she wasn't capable of making chase.

She turned and dragged her body painfully across the sand towards the cliff house. When she got closer, she looked up at it – at the dark, severe shape framed by the blue sky – and she knew that it had been waiting for her.

Not her. The other one.

19

Cassie stumbled in the kitchen doorway and steadied herself on the windowsill, but the edge of it crumbled away and smashed to the floor.

Fuck it again.

Now she saw that the wound on her injured hand had somehow reopened. The blood came out, not fast, but thick, and she let it. Looking closer, she was sure there were things crawling in it, like tiny insects, like when she'd once tried to grow a plant on her windowsill and she'd overwatered it and the water in the tray underneath it had become full of these little wriggling, white creatures.

She walked past the table and saw her untouched cup of tea still sitting there, cold and with a filmy layer on top and a dead fly floating in the middle. She went across the hallway, past Grandad Maddon's clock (tick-tock, tick-tock, still here) and into the sitting room and picked up the bottle of vodka from the drinks cabinet. First, she sloshed some over her bleeding hand and relished the burning pain. The vodka mixed with blood fell on Lucie's beautiful cabinet, but she didn't wash it off.

She closed her eyes in an attempt to ward off the flashes of memory that had been working their way through the torn covering of her brain for months now. Dark little mind-poems – doors that opened and then slammed shut. *Standing in the doorway to see Lucie staring at Bella with that same hard look on her face that she now saw in the photo, and Bella standing hunched, defiant, looking out from under her hair; Bella striding out of the sea, hands raw from the water, bruises down her leg from the rocks... marks on her arms; red hands, peeling claws; hateful eyes, a broken bust, a face in an ornate mirror that has slipped to one side so it's beautiful but it's at the wrong angle.*

Then, very deliberately, she lifted back her head and tipped a good half of the bottle down her throat. She spluttered and choked, her stomach burning and protesting. She felt the walls swaying, ever so slightly, like the house was teetering on the edge of something, ready to collapse.

She looked across at the mirror over the mantelpiece, and there was someone behind her.

Bella. It was all real, the whole time. It's not me. *I'm not sick. I'm not.*

She turned around quickly to catch the figure watching her, but as always, by the time she turned to face it, it had gone.

'Come back,' she said.

And then, very distinctly, from upstairs, came the sound of scratching.

But I got rid of them all.

She lurched towards the stairs and followed the sound, up, up, through the house, holding onto the banisters and dragging herself towards the attic, from where the sound was getting louder and louder. Halfway up the stairs, her feet went through one of the rotten boards and she had to wrench it out with her hands, only half registering the pain as the splinters ripped at her calf.

She pulled open the door to the attic stairs, and the scratching stopped in an instant. She swayed on the spot and held her re-opened wound to her chest. She *had* heard it. It *had* been there.

'Are you up there, Bella?' she called. And then: 'Shall I come up and play?'

And then there was another sound, this time from across the landing, from Lucie's room. She remembered Joe.

But I told him to go. I told him.

Leaving the attic behind her, she took herself back around the landing to the other side of the stairwell. She pushed open the door to Lucie's room.

Joe was lying on the floor in a mess of broken glass. A large, ragged shard from the broken mirror lay next to his hand to match the ragged gash across his throat. She stood there, transfixed, for a long moment and then moved a little further forward and bent down. The blood was coming from the wound in little spurts, bright red and viscous, not dark and coagulating like the wound on her hand. She leaned down and put her hand out to his rough, pockmarked face, and he opened his eyes and looked up at her.

'Lucie,' he said. 'Where...?'

She knelt down next to him and put her hand on him.

'No,' she said, 'Not her.'

Mrs Gibbett. She must have known he was up here earlier. She'd known it all along. That whole time they'd been talking in the kitchen, she'd known, because she was always watching and waiting, and this time she'd waited until Cassie had gone out to the beach and then she'd come in here... it was her, or it was something in this house...

Joe opened his mouth again. Something else bubbled from the depths of his torn throat, but whatever it was, she couldn't understand it.

'Oh God, what did you do, Cass?'

She stood up and turned to see Alex standing in the doorway.

'What do you mean, *what did I do*? Where did you go? Why are you back?'

'Joe...' said Alex.

She was staring at the man on the floor, and yet she didn't kneel down to help him. Neither of them did. He looked up at the two of them with helpless eyes. Cassie bent over and closed them like they did in films when people died so she didn't have to look at them anymore. He didn't resist.

What did you do? She shook Alex's question away and held on to the swaying doorframe again for support as she pulled herself back up. She took a final swig of the almost-empty bottle of vodka and let it fall to the floor.

'Joe and Lucie – they were...' She looked down at him again, and now his face was splitting into two. 'It was her all along, if you can believe it. Just Lucie. The two of them together – even while we were staying here, probably, all those years ago. It wasn't you, or me. Funny really, right?'

Alex shook her head. Her eyes were red but her voice, when it came out, was surprisingly decisive. 'He needs an ambulance.'

'I'm not lying, if that's what you think. It's all true. And there's more, too. About Bella and Lucie and...'

'You need help, Cass. I'm not the one who's struggling here; it's you. It's been you the whole time. I know about you, remember?' Her voice was softer now.

Cassie glanced over at the window now and saw, away in the distance over the flat landscape, flashing lights. Police. Ambulances. *And for all our problems, she was the only one I ought to have been able to trust.*

She turned back to Alex.

'You called them already. You already knew? Is this some kind of trap?'

'Cass, you're being paranoid. Look around you. Look at what's happening.'

It's going to be too late.

'Listen, Alex, quickly: I think Bella wants to punish me because I let it happen. But you can get away; it's not too late for you.'

'You didn't let anything happen. We were kids when we came here.'

Cassie looked out of the window again, and this time she saw Mrs Gibbett treading up the driveway. She glanced up and their eyes met.

Again, she turned to Alex, and now she clutched her arm. 'For fuck's sake, look, she's coming – see?'

Alex turned to look in the direction she was pointing in.

'She's known the whole time. She knows about everything that happened here and everything that Lucie did, and she doesn't care because she *worshipped* her. And she wants us out so she can have it all back to herself. I think she came in here and did this to Joe.'

From below, she heard the front door open and close. Then the heavy, unhurried footsteps coming up the stairs.

'Alex, listen to me, for once.'

She heard slow footsteps on the landing, a pause and then a sharp intake of breath behind her.

'Alexandra, I called the police like you asked.'

So they were in it together. She turned to face the woman, who'd stopped next to Alex in the doorway. She noticed that the chipped red nail polish had been cleaned away like it was never there. Cassie backed away from them both.

'Alex?'

'Cassandra, don't get upset. Your sister came to tell me she was worried about you, that's all. We're all *worried* about you. She thought it wasn't safe for you here, with him. And if you don't mind my saying so, you've been drinking, and now this...'

'I know everything. You can drop the harmless neighbour act.'

Mrs Gibbett's face transformed into a mask of hideous sympathy. 'Cassandra, you're upset. So many awful things have happened. Come on, let's get you both out of here; it's not right for us to be standing here like this. They'll help him when they come. They'll do what needs to be done.'

She nodded down to Joe.

'You knew, didn't you? About Joe and my aunt,' said Cassie.

Mrs Gibbett's face wrinkled up with distaste. 'Oh goodness, let's not go into that now. Your aunt might have tolerated him, but nothing more than that. Please.'

Cassie caught her breath for a moment. Lucie had been the one perfect, unassailable thing in her life, but she ought to have known it wasn't real. There is always the insect in the grass, the crab scuttling underneath the warm sand.

She's bad. Not her. The other one.

The people in that place they took her to, all those years ago when she was a young teenager after their summers here were over...

('Tell us what it is, Cassie. Can you tell us what is troubling you?'

'I don't know. I don't remember. Leave me alone.')

'I may be drunk but I'm not mad,' she said. 'Bella – she didn't drown by accident, did she?'

'I'm not listening to this,' said Alex. She went out onto the landing.

'Perhaps Lucie couldn't even help herself, the way she was with Bella, because – oh, sometimes all you can do is repeat what you knew yourself and nobody knows what it was like for her and our mother growing up with *him*.'

(Tick-tock, tick-tock, went the clock.)

Mrs Gibbett put a hand on her arm. Her voice was low and soothing and that was somehow more horrifying than anything else could have been. 'I didn't want to go into all this, but if you don't mind my saying, I think there are a lot of things you don't quite realise, Cassandra. Your cousin Bella was a bad girl as you know, and there's nothing wrong with a little punishment from a parent here and there. Your generation, you just don't understand about discipline. You shouldn't do this and you shouldn't do that and the poor little innocents need to have their feelings listened to. Only, what if they don't *have* feelings?' This last part came out like a low hiss. 'Some of them don't, you know, whatever they might say these days. And your aunt – well, it was a privilege to me to help her in any way I could. She had a lot to cope with in that girl.'

'What did Lucie do?' she said. 'What did *you* do?'

Mrs Gibbett leaned closer to her.

'I did what I always did. I helped your aunt clear up the mess, and I'll help you now.' She nodded to Joe. 'You see, she trusted me...' She shook her head, and as she did, she glanced at the crumbling bust of the woman on the floor, where it had fallen after the mirror smashed. She stepped over Joe – casually, like he was a pile of clothes – and gently straightened it. When she turned around, she spoke in a clear, unnaturally bright voice.

'Come on, I mean it now. You've both had a terrible shock. There's nothing we can do for him. You must come outside with me.'

She held out her hand, and then, somehow, they were all three standing out on the landing, only she didn't remember how they had got there and she didn't know if Alex had even heard their conversation. It felt dark, even though it was still the middle of a summer's day and she knew outside the sun was still beating down and it would never stop. Something moved next to her. She turned to the long mirror in the hallway, and now the face that looked back at her was only Bella's, no Lucie; but this Bella was rotten and bloated and choked up. Hate burned out of her eyes, because out of all of them *Cassie was the one who knew.* When Bella ripped things apart, had it been just so she could see what was inside, if anything? Would she rip Cassie apart so she could see inside her? (Or had she, in fact, already succeeded?)

'So you *have* been here this whole time,' she said. 'I knew it.'

She could hear the scratching clearer than ever, like hundreds of creatures scraping at the walls and slowly but surely eating away at the house (*at her mind?*) until what was left would be only a shell.

Cassie stumbled back from Mrs Gibbett's reaching arms.

'Get away from me, I don't want to go anywhere with you.' She turned to her sister. 'Alex, I mean it: go away while you still can and don't come back. Can't you see her?'

'Who, Cass?'

'I mean, can't you see what's been happening here, in this house?'

Alex bit her lip.

'But who said anything about going anywhere, Cassandra? This is where you belong, it's what your aunt left to you. Don't you worry about a thing: I'll take care of you, just like I took care of her. We just need to step outside for a bit, and then once – once this is all over, you can come back home. The police are here – no, don't look back at him, we'll sort that out. Everything will be fine, you'll see.'

Low, soothing voice, rough hand reaching out to her in all confidence that she would take it.

Alex came round to the other side of her, and she allowed herself to be led unsteadily away from the room, along the landing, past the long mirror. Out of the corner of her eye, she watched the Lucie-Bella-her walk alongside her, or what was left of her.

Down the stairs, past the ticking clock, through the kitchen and out the door. She saw the doors to the ambulance that had just parked outside open and three people emerge from it. There were a couple of police cars behind the ambulance and she saw people getting out of them, too. *Come for him? Come for me? Doesn't matter either way.*

It was all going to be fine, that's what Mrs Gibbett said. And there was something like triumph behind those eyes, which made Cassie think, *She's won. She has what she wants. Cassie's sick. Cassie will admit she is sick and she will stay here and get sicker and more helpless and she will never be able to leave just like Lucie couldn't leave in the end. Otherwise, she'll tell.*

There was something in front of the wheels of the ambulance, and for a moment, she thought, *they've killed a child.* Then she saw it was a doll. An old, dirty baby doll with its face crushed beyond recognition into the dry dirt, but there was more than that too, because mixed in with the bits of broken doll face and arms, she could see blood and claws and placenta. She tried to blink it all away and then looked past the cars to the road, further down, where she saw a lone figure with red hair walking away, head bowed like she was crying.

'Come this way, Cassie,' she heard either Alex or Mrs Gibbett say, but she ignored them and turned her face away from them towards the end of garden, the eroding cliff edge where Lucie had fallen, and that's when she saw her: Bella. All of her. Not a face in a mirror – not a figure from a distance. Even from this distance, she could see those pale blue eyes boring into her and she met them, and something froze in her, and they stared at each other for a long moment.

'I'm sorry,' Cassie told her. 'Is that what you want to hear? I'm sorry.'

'What is it, Cass?' said Alex, shaking her arm. 'Who are you talking to?'

She turned to her sister.

'I do care, you know.'

'I know. We can make things better, Cass. Like you said, it's not too late. Please?'

There were people getting out of the police cars in the driveway now and walking towards them. Bella didn't care that she was sorry. And that's when Cassie finally knew exactly why Lucie had come back here in the end, because it was the same for her. She was pulled here by an irresistible, invisible thread of guilt attached to her. You can't escape your past. Those claws dig in and hold fast and they reach into the future, too.

But no. You can escape them if you want to.

With all her remaining strength, Cassie pushed them away from her and half ran, half stumbled around the back of the house, through the garden and towards the edge of the crumbling cliff. She heard Alex calling to her but she kept going and the seagulls circled crazily overhead and she felt exulted, more powerful than she had for years. Like she could fly.

And then she was lying amongst the jagged rocks on the beach at the foot of the cliff, looking up towards the house, hearing nothing but a ringing in her ears. Something was trickling down the side of her head, and she tried to lift her arm to touch it but her arm wouldn't work. Neither would her legs. Curiously, she felt nothing. No pain, where there should have been pain; no fear, where there should have been fear. No tingling anymore, no burning – she was free of it all.

Two faces appeared over the edge of the cliff and looked down at her and she saw that one of them was Alex and she had fallen to her knees, but her eyes travelled past them and up to the house to fix on the window at the top of the landing, where another face was looking down at her, only it was too far away to tell which of them it was. And along with the ringing in her ears was the sound of soft piano music, so she closed her eyes to listen to it.

No need to be sorry anymore.

Next to her, where she lay, there were marks like lesions in the sand. And then they came; they came and they began to crawl all over her, and she let them. She smiled, and then the smile turned into a laugh, and the sea breeze caught it and took it away.

Epilogue

In the big house on the cliff, a heavy-set woman shuffles from room to room, every day the same route, dusting, stroking the furniture, shaking her head when she sees that another crack has appeared in a wall or on a ceiling. If anybody was there with her, they might now and then hear her talking softly.

'I always knew that girl was trouble,' she says, or 'It wasn't your fault – it wasn't your fault at all. Don't worry, I'll look after you now. I'm not going anywhere.'

And now and then, from the attic, there is a clawing, clawing, which she either doesn't hear or pretends not to hear. Tick-tock, goes the grandfather clock.

***

Elsewhere is another person who is stronger than her appearance suggests. She sits in the bedroom of her rented flat with a photo on her lap of four people on the beach: a woman with her arms around two girls; another girl standing just off frame. Deliberately, she pulls out a pen and crosses out the face of the woman. She does it again, and again, harder and harder, until it is not a face anymore. Before putting the picture down, she pauses for a moment to stroke the face of the taller girl and then she plants a kiss on it. Free now, at least. At peace. Or that's what she chooses to believe.

Someone is calling to her from the next room. She gets up and pulls her delicate shoulders back and walks out on bare feet which are small but strong and supple. She will not stay in the past, because she knows that if she does, they will pull her in after them. And that will not happen to her.

She is going to live.

Author Profile

Victoria Hattersley lives in Norwich, UK and studied English Literature at the University of East Anglia. She was brought up in the Fens of East Anglia, where the sky is intimidatingly vast and the ground is gradually sinking. This may account for her upbeat writing style. She has a long-held love of the Gothic which she has never been able to shake and very likely never will.

She lives with her daughter, cats and expanding book collection. It is her ambition to age into Miss Havisham (though not to burn to death in her own house).

https://victoriahattersley.com

Twitter - VicLHattersley

Instagram - victoriahattersley_writer

What Did You Think of
What Was Left of Her?

A big thank you for purchasing this book. It means a lot that you chose this book specifically from such a wide range on offer. I do hope you enjoyed it.

Book reviews are incredibly important for an author. All feedback helps them improve their writing for future projects and for developing this edition. If you are able to spare a few minutes to post a review on Amazon, that would be much appreciated.

Publisher Information

Rowanvale Books provides publishing services to independent authors, writers and poets all over the globe. We deliver a personal, honest and efficient service that allows authors to see their work published, while remaining in control of the process and retaining their creativity. By making publishing services available to authors in a cost-effective and ethical way, we at Rowanvale Books hope to ensure that the local, national and international community benefits from a steady stream of good quality literature.

For more information about us, our authors or our publications, please get in touch.

www.rowanvalebooks.com
info@rowanvalebooks.com

Printed in Great Britain
by Amazon

27644088R00085